The Secret Pledge

Episodes 1 to 3

By: Molly McDunn

CONTENTS

Molly McDunn

This book is a work of fiction. The characters, incidents, and dialogue are drawn from the author's imagination and are not to be construed as real. Any resemblance to actual events or persons, living or dead, is entirely coincidental.

ISBN: 978-0-9738879-7-6

Tovuti Publishing
230 – 1210 Summit Drive,
Kamloops, BC V2C 6M1
Canada

EPISODE 1

ONE

Julia pulled a box, dusty with age, into the middle of the attic floor.

She had little energy to be emptying the home she and Kevin had bought together five years earlier, but as a newly divorced woman living on a teacher's salary she couldn't afford the English Tudor tucked away on the North Shore of Long Island. And Kevin—well, he'd told her he wanted to sell it.

"We'll probably break even," he'd said.

Divorced. Julia never thought that word would pass her lips when referring to herself. She and Kevin had such hopes for the future.

"Julia!" her mother called from the floor below. "Do you plan on taking the shower curtain and rugs in here?"

"In here" had to mean the bathroom.

"I hadn't really thought about it!" Julia called back. She paused, mentally recalling the small apartment she'd be moving into. It had a shower stall, but no full bath.

She shouted, "No, no, I don't want them."

Her voice cracked in spite of the fact she was trying to remain strong. After all, how could she crumble in front of her mother, a woman who never married again after her husband, Julia's father, died?

That's when it occurred to her that she had a box somewhere in the attic of stuff she'd taken when helping her mother move from the Cape Cod they'd lived in to the apartment her mother now lived in. Her mother downsized not long after Julia married Kevin.

Funny how she just remembered now about a photo she'd seen of the man she knew had to be her father, but hadn't said anything about it at the time since she was too caught up in her impending marriage. The photo wouldn't be in the box she'd just pulled out.

She looked around, shoving bags of stuffed animals out of the way that had been from her childhood and bent down, looking in the corners until she spotted the small box.

She was on a deadline to get out of the house so that the new people could do a walk through before going to closing, but she needed a break; more importantly, she needed a distraction.

She went over to the corner, sat down and put the box on her lap. She'd never mentioned to her mother that she had taken it and her mother had never asked its whereabouts. Julia figured she'd forgotten about it.

She opened the box and remembered that it held more than just a picture, but also keepsakes from her father's childhood. She riffled through it, finding a Boy Scout's badge, a funky looking seashell and a key.

She wondered if it was the only key for some special place and started to imagine just what that could be when she came across the photo.

Her father had to be a teenager in it, but he was standing next to an older looking woman, his arm wrapped around her waist. Julia looked on the back. "Katherine, the love of my life" was scribbled on it.

Julia's mother's name was Ellen, and just then Julia heard Ellen climbing up the creaky ladder steps.

"Honey," Ellen said, "are you staying here tonight? If not I can pack up your shampoo and..." She reached the top step and walked into the attic. She hesitated, before saying, "What's that?"

Julia looked up, feeling as though she'd been caught stealing. And maybe that is what it was. She sputtered, trying to close up the box, "I...I...I just took a break. Sorry."

"Why are you sorry?" Ellen said, walking closer.

Julia's eyes filled with tears. "I don't know. I just am."

Ellen crouched down. She reached over, pulling the box from her daughter's grasp. "How'd this end up here? I thought it somehow got tossed out when I moved."

It was the first time Julia noticed how old her mother was getting. The blue in her eyes had dulled and the gray in her hair was now all white. Julia had been so consumed the last few years by her own trials that she hadn't paid attention to the woman who sacrificed everything for her.

"Julia?" her mother prodded.

"I took it, Mom," she said. "I was going to ask you about it, but then everything just got busy and I forgot about it until now."

"I see you found Katherine," she said. "The love of your father's life."

Julia gazed at her mother. "I don't understand. She looks old enough to be--"

"His mother? I guess it wouldn't have been impossible."

"But this was before you?"

Ellen nodded. "I met your father several years after this was taken."

"Did she break his heart?" Julia asked.

Ellen shook her head. "In a way. She died in a car accident."

Julia gasped. The woman looked to be about her age. To think that life could end so quickly, changing the direction of the lives of others suddenly became very real. Then again, it was something her mother was quite aware of.

"I always wondered why I never knew Dad's family," Julia said. "It's as though they never existed."

Ellen picked up the picture, staring at it. "They live just outside of Philadelphia." She flushed a deep red and quickly added, "I mean, they did. Who knows where they are now."

"You didn't know them, did you?"

"No. Your father, well, he wasn't very close with them."

"It's weird," Julia said.

"What do you mean?"

"Well, there's a whole side of my family—my bloodline—that I don't even know. I mean, what if they have medical information that could have helped."

"Who said it's you?" Ellen snapped. "Who said it was your fault you couldn't get pregnant? Maybe it was Kevin's issue."

Julia shrugged. "I don't know, I always just figured it had to be me." Tears began to stream down her face. "I always thought as we got older, things would be easier, that the questions would be answered."

Ellen brushed back a strand of Julia's blonde hair from her face. "Not quite."

"Mom, do you think maybe sometimes you protected me too much while I was growing up?"

Her mother had attended every sport event Julia participated in, every competition. Unlike other mothers who had to work and couldn't be such an active part of their child's life, Ellen was always there.

She'd told Julia that she needed to fill the shoes of two parents without explaining how she managed to do so without bringing in an income.

Ellen said, "Maybe I did overprotect you, sweetie, but I did what I had to do. You were my life."

Just then, for some reason, Julia had a strong yearning to get to know as much as she could about her father.

Her mother only said wonderful things about him. She kept their wedding photo on the end table and never brought home another man. She always referred to her husband as "the love of her life."

But after seeing what was written on the back of the photo, Julia wondered if that was a phrase she used specifically.

"Mom, I want to go meet Dad's family."

"No," Ellen said. "That just can't happen."

"Why?"

"It's just not a good idea. You're feeling, well, vulnerable right now. Why stir things up?"

"Stir things up? Mom, you know more than you're letting on."

"No, no, that's not it," Ellen said, wringing her hands. "It's just, well, they aren't warm people."

Julia studied her mother for a moment. "So you do know them."

Ellen sighed as if in resignation. "Not really." She stopped for a moment, selecting her words carefully. "See, your father went to tell them in person that I was pregnant. He hadn't seen them in years after he left and he felt that the news would be what would heal their relationship."

"But they never came to your wedding. Why would he think that your being pregnant would do it?"

"Time, sweetheart. Time changes things."

"I can't believe you never met his family. Why didn't you go with Dad when he went to tell them?"

"Well, first, I was too sick. I didn't have just morning sickness, but morning, noon and night sickness for the first several months. Besides, he wasn't sure how they would react and he didn't want me to be there if it didn't go well."

Julia closed up the box. "Well, since time does change things, I think I will go look for my other family. I need to find something to get my mind off of my troubles. School's on break and I have some time."

"I really wish you wouldn't," Ellen said.

"Why?" Julia asked, raising her voice.

"Because...because something tells me you're going to be disappointed with what you find out."

"Just add it to my list," Julia said.

"Come on, Julia, this isn't a good idea. Besides, you'll be busy with moving and setting up your new place. This just isn't a good idea."

"For who, Mom?"

TWO

Three weeks later, with the house sold and all Julia's belongings now in her apartment, she was heading toward Philadelphia in her blue Jetta.

She'd booked a room in the heart of Philadelphia. A Google search informed her that there were several people with the surname of Kolson living in the Philadelphia area.

She'd been a Kolson before marrying Kevin and she may just take the name back, depending on how she was greeted by her dad's family.

She thought maybe a higher power was giving her a signal of some sort when she drove past a billboard stating Dale Kolson for Assemblyman. She wondered if it were possible that the politician was related to her father.

After the three-hour ride from Long Island, she checked into the Marriott. It was around two pm on a Tuesday.

She collapsed on the bed, realizing that she didn't really have a plan. Her mother didn't give her much information at all.

When Julia called her the night before to try to get as many details as possible before taking the trip, her mother's response wasn't terribly satisfactory:

"Your father didn't talk about them, Julia. They just weren't a part of our lives."

"How could you let him get away with that, Mom?" Julia shouted into the phone. "Weren't you curious to know his family?"

"I don't know. Whenever I asked about them he made it clear it was a subject he wasn't comfortable talking about."

"That doesn't make sense!"

"Not now, it doesn't, but I was in love with your father. He was all I needed."

Then something occurred to her. "But you had to have met them at the funeral. They had to have come to his funeral."

Ellen paused. "No. I was told that they couldn't because of the investigation."

"Investigation? You said it was a hunting accident. Why was there---"

"There's always an investigation, Julia, whenever there's a gun involved."

"How come you never told me that, Mom? How come---"

"Enough with the questions, Julia!" Ellen snapped. "I'm too tired for all this. Just too tired! Why do you have to go and stir things up?" She then hung up the phone.

Julia sat up on the edge of the bed, her stomach growling. That's when she realized she'd missed lunch. She decided to get a bite to eat before beginning her search. She freshened up and went down to the lobby, asking the concierge for a recommendation for casual dining. He suggested a pub that was three blocks down the street.

***

"We don't have table service right now," a host said when Julia walked in, "but you could order something from the bar."

Julia looked over to see that it was empty, which was just as well with her. She went over and pulled up a stool, the bartender, a gray-haired gentleman, asked what he could get for her. "Could I have a menu?' she said. "And a Sprite?"

A short time later, she was enjoying a burger with some fries, and small talk with Ron, the bartender. Finally, he asked what brought her to Philly from "da Island." He exaggerated "da Island" when he said it and then laughed.

"Yeah, I guess we do talk funny," Julia said.

"Nah, don't take me seriously. But you here on business or for pleasure?"

Julia took a sip of her soda before saying, "I guess a bit of both. I'm trying to find some long lost relatives."

"That right?"

"Yeah, you wouldn't know anyone by the name Kolson, would you?"

He stopped and studied her for a minute. "Who sent you in here?"

"What do you mean?"

"Don't play games with me. Why don't you pay your bill and be on your way."

Julia swallowed hard. "No one sent me here," she said. "I'm just---"

"Hey, Ron." A voice came from the end of the bar. "Cut her some slack, would you? She may be on the up and up."

Julia looked down to see a guy who appeared to be in his thirties, dirty blond hair. When had he come in? He shot her a warm smile. "Name's Jack," he said. He glanced at Ron. "Pour me a cold one."

Keeping a scowl on Julia, Ron went to one of the taps and poured out a Guinness, bringing it to Jack.

Julia said, "Listen, I don't know why you are so upset. I never knew my father or his family." She pushed her plate away, no longer feeling hungry. "But should I be worried?"

Jack shifted down the bar, closer to Julia. "The name's Kolson, huh?"

"Yes. My dad's name was Dennis."

Jack and Ron exchanged glances. "Dennis Kolson?" Jack said.

Julia nodded while keenly aware Ron was paying close attention to her.

"He died here about thirty years ago."

"Out hunting with his brothers," Ron sneered.

"Brothers?" Julia said.

"Dale and Donald," Jack said.

"Is that the same Dale as the one running for office?" Julia said. "Dale Kolson?"

Jack and Ron both snickered with Jack adding, "You could say that."

"Wow, so would you know how I could find him? I just need to meet some family."

"Listen, sweetie," Ron said, "you'd be better to head back home and forget this. They're not the family type."

"Let her be, Ron," Jack said. Then to Julia, he added, "How about I show you where his headquarters is?"

"Um," Julia said, "I don't really know you and it's not a good idea for me to--"

Jack threw some money on the bar. "I got hers," he said, pointing to Julia's plate. "Ms. Kolson, I was only going to walk you the few blocks from here. I wouldn't ask you to get in my car, me being a complete stranger and all."

"It's Julia," she said, putting out her hand, feeling herself blush. "Julia Barnes."

"Married name?" Jack said.

"Used to be," she said. "I'm divorced now."

Jack nodded, a smile playing on his lips. "So, do you trust walking with me or would you prefer to take the stroll on your own?"

She thought about it for a moment. "I don't want to take up any of your time."

Jack shrugged. "I have nowhere to be. Besides, this guy here can vouch for me. I'm not any sort of crook."

"That's right," Ron said. "He's not a Kolson."

THREE

Several minutes later, they turned on to Walnut Street. Jack said, "It's down there on the left. You'll see the sign in the window."

"Oh," Julia said. "Okay."

"It's better they don't see me with you," he said.

"I get the feeling they can't be trusted," Julia said.

"Just play it cool," Jack said, turning and walking back toward where they come from. Julia wanted to ask if she'd see him again, but stopped herself. What did it matter?

She headed toward the building where there was a huge sign in the window that read DALE KOLSON: WORKING FOR YOU! blocking her from seeing what was going on inside. Taking a deep breath, she opened the door to hear the warning buzzer. A heavyset woman sitting behind a desk looked up at her.

"May I help you?"

"I'm looking for Dale Kolson."

The woman grabbed a notepad. "Name."

"Excuse me?"

The woman looked up over the top of her glasses resting on her nose. "Your name."

"Oh, Julia. Julia Barnes."

"Uh, huh, and this is in reference to…" Her words came out in a sing song tone.

"He doesn't know me, but…" Her mouth went dry as she blurted, "But his brother was my father."

The woman sat ramrod straight. "Donald's your father?"

"No, no, Dennis. His brother Dennis."

"Dennis? You must have the wrong person. They don't have a brother named Dennis."

"Well, he died. About thirty years ago."

The woman scowled, and then seemed to gather herself before saying, "Did you want to leave a number where Mr. Kolson can reach you?"

Julia nodded. "Yes, I'm staying at the Marriott, but he can call my cell phone."

"Excellent," the woman said, after taking down Julia's number, "I'll give him the message."

"Do you know when he'll be back?"

"Back? Here?" the woman said. "Well, he's rarely here." She hesitated, then added, "He…he likes to be among the people."

Julia nodded, thanked the woman and walked out, hoping that Dale Kolson would get in touch with her, even though there was an element of unease in her gut. Maybe I should just go back home and forget the whole thing, she thought, as she strolled down the block, heading back toward the hotel. She looked at her cell phone, making sure it was on. It was.

"So, get any answers?"

She jumped and turned to see Jack standing there.

She heaved a sigh of relief, realizing just how on edge she was. "Not really," she said. "He wasn't there."

"Not surprised," Jack said.

"Jack, obviously the Kolsons have some sort of reputation. And it's not good. Can you fill me in?"

He waited for a moment, and then said, "How about I take you to dinner tonight? Eight o'clock. We can talk then."

"I guess."

"Don't sound so thrilled," Jack said.

"No, it's not that," Julia said, watching passersby glance their way. "It's just if he calls and wants to meet, I'd hate to stand you up, but I really want to--"

"I know, I know," Jack said. "Here's where I can be reached," he said, handing her a business card that read Jack Landry, Freelance Journalist. It included his phone number.

Julia looked up at him. "You're a reporter? Who do you write for?"

He nodded at the card. "Freelancer. I write for whoever's paying. So, if you don't hear from him by seven, let's make this a date. I'll pick you up at 7:30 in the lobby. Okay?" At Julia's nod, he turned and walked in the opposite direction.

FOUR

"I hope you like steak," Jack said, as they walked into a restaurant that was more elegant than Julia dressed for.

Pointing to her white slacks and black top, she said, "This is as dressy as I could be with what I packed," she said.

When Jack had picked her up wearing a nice blazer and khakis, she realized they'd be going someplace nice. She just hadn't expected it to be quite as nice as it was.

She felt the hostess giving her the once over as she led them to their table, which was off in the corner.

"You look great," Jack said.

"You're kind," Julia replied. Truth was, Kevin hadn't complimented her in years, in spite of her trim figure, and she wasn't sure how to handle one now. She slid into the banquette, assuming Jack was going to take the chair across from her, but instead he slid in next to her. He smelled nice.

When the hostess handed them their menus, Jack said, "I hope you're not vegan."

She smiled. "No. I tried once, but it only lasted a day, if that."

Jack laughed. "I hear their French onion soup is the best in Philly."

"So, you've never been here before?" Julia said, opening the menu. She gave an audible gasp.

"What's wrong?" Jack said.

"It's so expensive!" she said.

Jack glanced down at his menu and she thought she detected a look of horror. "You didn't realize it, did you?"

"It's only money," Jack said.

"We could share something," Julia replied.

"No, no, no. This is fine."

"But a baked potato is nine dollars, Jack," she muttered.

"I said don't worry about it." Jack looked up and began scanning the restaurant. Julia figured he'd never return and wanted to take in the ambiance while he could.

It was rather glamorous, she had to admit, with an old Hollywood feel. Well, the Hollywood she saw in classic movies that she and Kevin used to enjoy together.

That's when it dawned on her that she hadn't thought much about her divorce since she'd arrived in Philadelphia.

"How about we get the porterhouse for two?" Jack said.

"Sure." Julia wasn't feeling very hungry anyway. Her mind was on getting as much information from Jack as possible.

When the waitress came over, Jack ordered for the both of them, including the soup. When they were asked what they wanted to drink, Julia said that water would suffice.

"Oh, come on," Jack said. "How about a nice full-bodied red to go with the steak? You do like wine, right?"

She did.

Jack ordered a bottle from the menu, but Julia didn't get a chance to see how much it cost before the hostess took back the menus and walked away.

"Okay," Jack said, leaning in. "I know you wanted to pick my brain, but I'd first like to get to know you before I spill my guts."

"What do you want to know?"

"Well, for starters, you said earlier you're divorced. Are there any children in the mix?"

Julia looked down. It was as though he'd taken one of the steak knives on the table and stabbed her in the heart. "No," she said. "No children. We actually just sold our house and I'm trying to pick up the pieces."

"I guess it's a good thing then that there aren't any children," Jack said.

How could he know that was the major reason for the divorce? Julia willed herself not to cry.

"And what do you do...for a living?" he said.

"I'm a teacher. I teach eighth grade math."

Jack nodded. "That's a respectable job."

"I like it. The kids are great and I get summers off, which is why I have the time to be here in Philade—Philly."

The inquisition continued. "Do you have any siblings?"

"No. My mom never remarried after my father died."

"Dennis."

Julia looked up. "Yes, Dennis. Dennis Kolson. The secretary today didn't seem to know there was a third brother."

"I'm not surprised," Jack said. "They probably would rather no one knew."

Just then the waitress appeared with a bottle of wine. She uncorked it and poured a sample in Jack's glass. He took a sip and said it was fine. After the waitress poured each a glass, placed the bottle on the table, and walked away, Jack leaned over to Julia and whispered, "I wouldn't know if it was good or not, I'm a Guinness man."

Julia laughed. "That I knew. From the bar today, which leads me to ask, why was Ron so upset?"

Jack raised an eyebrow. "Well, that's really Ron's story to tell, but let's just say that the Kolsons have had their eyes on that property for some time and if they get their way, they'll succeed in the not-too-faraway future."

Julia mulled it over, and then said, "But what I don't understand is why you are investing so much money in this meal when all I want is some information. A coffee shop would've been fine and it would've been my treat. I can afford a cup of coffee, but certainly not these prices."

He leaned in close again. "I'm thinking of this as a date, even if you aren't."

It was the first "date" she'd had since she and Kevin's marriage ended. Kevin, on the other hand, was seriously involved with someone else, which was what stunned her the most when he said he wanted a divorce.

At first he blamed the fact that they hadn't been able to start a family, but then mentioned something about finding someone he believed he was falling in love with. Julia didn't think she'd ever be able to trust another man after that.

The idea caused her to look at Jack and ask, "Besides, what about you? Were you married? Are you married?"

Jack shook his head. "Nope. No children either." He took a plentiful sip of his wine, as though it were a cold beer and not a fine Cabernet.

French onion soups were placed in front of them and they began to eat. "Wow," Julia said, "this is good."

"It'd better be."

"So, do you think you can talk and eat at the same time?" Julia said.

Jack patted his mouth with his cloth napkin, and said, "A bit of back story for you. The Kolsons are very well known in this town. They go back a couple of generations. David Kolson, that's Dale and Donald's father---"

"Wait, do they have something for the letter D?"

Jack laughed. "Want to know what David's wife's name is?"

"Diane...Doreen," Julia said.

Jack shook his head and laughed. "Susan. Apparently, women don't play a major part in these guys' lives. Anyway, Susan died a few years back so it is just the Kolson men wreaking havoc on this great town of ours."

"In what way?"

"For one, politics."

"But assemblyman? That isn't that powerful of a position, is it?" Julia said.

"You have to start somewhere without it looking too obvious. Their father owns Kolson Petroleum, as well as other businesses. Most not under the name Kolson. Anyway, when David wanted to keep his family looking lily white and with two boys--" He stopped himself, and then added, "Three boys, it wasn't easy."

Jack went mum when one of the wait staff picked up their empty bowls. Once they were out of earshot, he continued. "For years there've been rumors about the power this family has, but without any proof, who's to say? The Kolsons chalk it up to jealousy."

"You seem to know a lot about these people."

"None of what I told you is news, except to you. Although, I am curious to know what Dale will think when he gets your message," he said with a shrug.

The entrees were delivered. Julia admitted that the steak was tender as butter. She noticed, though, that Jack seemed distracted, constantly looking around the room. She wished he paid more attention to her, his ostensible date.

While they ate, Jack filled her in on some of the properties that the family owned and the organizations they were involved with. None of it revealed anything to her, though, about her father. With the last bite, she said, "I just wish I could talk to someone about my father. That's all I want."

Suddenly, Jack straightened and motioned with a nod. "See who just walked in?"

Julia looked across the room where two men, nattily dressed in business suits, both with elegant women at their side, seemed to be bantering with the maitre d'.

"Just what I was hoping for," Jack said.

"Who are they?"

"That's Donald Kolson."

Julia jumped up, to get a better look, but Jack immediately pulled her back down. "Don't let them see you!"

"Why?" she said.

"Because, because they value their privacy." He shifted off to the side, as if hiding himself.

"Which one's Donald?"

"He's on the left, your left. That's his wife. She is very involved with the community. Looks like they're dining with the Singers. That's Reginald and Molly Singer. They are very powerful people here, too."

Julia watched as they followed the maitre d' to see where they were going to be seated, but they went out of her line of vision. "How can I introduce myself? I can't just walk up to their table."

"True. Besides, they're probably dining privately. In the back."

"I didn't get a good look, either."

The waitress appeared with dessert menus. "Everyone loves our baked Alaska, but feel free to see what some of our other delightful offerings are."

Julia was stuffed and had no interest in adding to the pricey meal, but she wasn't ready to leave just yet either. Not when there was some way she could meet her father's brother.

"I'll be back after you've had a chance to look everything over," the waitress said before departing.

"Jack, I don't want dessert," she said.

"But you don't want to leave now, either, huh?"

She nodded.

"Well, look, we still have more wine to finish. Why don't we take our time and enjoy it?"

She smiled. "That's a good idea." Still, it didn't mean she'd get the opportunity she was looking for. She said, "I'm going to the ladies room. I'll be right back."

She started to slide out of the banquette when Jack grasped her by the arm. "Julia, you can't go up to his table. They'll throw you right out of here."

"I won't. I promise. I really need to go."

Jack let go of her arm. She got up and had to ask one of the waiters where the restroom was. Unfortunately, it was the opposite side of the direction she wanted to go.

She used the facility and while washing her hands and freshening her lipstick she hoped that at least one of the women with the Kolson party would come in.

Julia would find a way to let them know who she was. Certainly, they would convey the message to Donald Kolson! But, they didn't come in and Julia had to return to the table disappointed. She sat down next to Jack.

"Don't look so sad," Jack said.

"Do you know both your parents, Jack?" she said.

He nodded, scowling. "They've been married for close to forty years now."

"You have family on both sides? Know them well?"

He studied her. "Yes..."

The waitress appeared. "So, have we decided what to have?"

"We're passing on dessert," Jack said. "But, I'm wondering if you could do me a favor?"

The waitress stood in anticipation.

"I want to buy a round of drinks for Mr. Kolson and his friends and have it put on my bill. And please say that it is from—Julia Kolson, his niece."

The waitress said, "Julie Kolson, his niece."

"Julia," both Jack and Julia corrected.

"Very good, sir. I'll bring you your check shortly."

Julia stared at Jack. "I'll pay for those drinks."

"Don't worry about it. It'll be fun to see how he reacts."

With the bill sitting next to Jack, they nursed their drinks, waiting for Donald to appear out of curiosity.

When the waitress returned, Jack asked if she'd delivered the drinks and message. She said she had, but that they weren't the only ones buying rounds of drinks for the table. "It's always the same whenever they are here. Everyone wants to get in their good favor and buys them rounds. You're just one of many."

Jack slipped a credit card in the bill holder and handed it to the waitress. "We're done here."

***

It was around one in the morning. Julia laid in her hotel bed mentally going over her day and evening. Who were these people that were her father's family? They were obviously powerful, but her mother never gave the implication that she knew any such thing.

32

She rolled over on her side, her thoughts switching to Jack. She couldn't imagine how much the bill cost, but when she tried to help pay for it, he wouldn't hear of it.

Then as they headed back to the hotel she wondered if he was expecting payment in her bed, but instead of inviting himself up to her room he kissed her on the cheek and said he'd be calling the next day.

She didn't think she would be able to fall asleep, but she had; however, it wasn't long before she was awakened by her cell phone ringing. She tried to adjust her eyes to see the number, but when that didn't work she just answered.

"Who are you and what do you want?" a voice said.

"Excuse me?" she mumbled.

"If you're trying to pull something, be warned." It was a man's voice. "Blackmailers never win."

Blackmailers? "Wait, is this Donald or Dale?"

"Never mind who it is. Just leave them alone, got it?"

"But you don't understand! I'm Dennis's daughter."

Silence.

"Hello?" Julia said, now fully awake. "Hello?"

Whoever it was had hung up. When she looked more closely at her phone's screen she saw that the number had been blocked.

Of course.

FIVE

Julia called Jack the next morning, but he didn't pick up. She left him a message about the strange phone message she'd received and then as an afterthought thanked him again for the dinner.

When he didn't return her call by noon, she began to panic. What had happened to him? She was sure that he would have been concerned.

There was a knock at her hotel room door. Julia stood stock still. What if they came to do her harm?

"Housekeeping."

Sighing with relief, Julia ran over and peered through the peephole to see a woman with a cart. She opened the door, and said, "I'm fine."

"Clean towels?"

"No, I have enough."

"Sorry to disturb you."

"No worries," Julia said, admonishing herself for not putting the do not disturb sign on the door handle. She thanked the woman and closed the door just as her cell phone rang. She dashed over to the nightstand. It was a number she didn't recognize, but it wasn't blocked so she answered it.

"Julia!" Jack said. "I just got your message."

"Oh, thank goodness you're okay."

"I was called on an assignment this morning. There was a situation over at one of the high schools."

"Oh, okay. What did you think about the messa---"

"How about I show you around town today?" Jack said, cutting her off.

"I don't know if that's---"

"There's so much to see and since you'll be leaving soon, I didn't want you to go without---"

Leaving soon?

"I'll be there in about a half hour. Meet me out front," he said, and then just hung up.

She thought he sounded strange, but showered and dressed in a pair of jeans and sleeveless pink blouse as quickly as possible. By the time she slapped a minimum amount of makeup on, she was due to be in the lobby. When she got there, Jack was waiting for her.

"You look beautiful," he said, approaching her and kissing her on the lips. Keeping his voice low, he said, "My car's out front."

Once they got in his Rav 4 and turned onto the street, he said, "I didn't want to take any chances after that strange phone call you got." He glanced in his rearview and side mirrors.

"You think I'm in danger?" Julia said, wide-eyed.

"You were threatened, weren't you?"

All she wanted was to get to know her father somehow.

"Listen, I was thinking," Jack said, keeping his hand on the wheel, "by any chance the threat could be from your ex or someone he is associated with?"

"Kevin?" she said. "Not at all. He couldn't wait to get the divorce papers signed and house sold. No, that wasn't something Kevin would've done." She paused for a moment, and then added, "But I don't want you put in the middle of this, Jack."

"I won't let that happen," he said.

"Where are we going?"

"The zoo."

"The zoo?"

"Yeah, let's get lost in the crowd."

***

Not much later, Julia and Jack were inside the zoo sitting on a bench and chowing down on some hot dogs. It was the first meal that day for Julia and she was appreciating every morsel.

Once they finished eating, Jack said, "Do you remember exactly what you said to the secretary at the Kolson office?"

"Just what I told you yesterday."

"There's something about your father's death that has them scared, I think." He stood. "I do better thinking while walking. Come on, let's check out the gorillas."

While they were watching Kuchimba knuckle-walking around the exhibit scrounging for food, Jack looked to be deep in thought. Julia waited for him to speak. Finally, he did.

"Are you sure your mom never met these people?"

Julia shrugged. "That's what she told me."

"But wouldn't she have met them at your father's funeral?"

"That's what I asked her, but she said they sent his body home after the shooting and they didn't come because of some investigation."

"Excuse me?"

"I know!" Julia said. "But when I pushed her for more details, she said she didn't want to talk about it anymore." Julia turned to Jack, and added, "Do you think they threatened her?"

Jack shrugged. "Probably."

"But all I want to know---"

"What you want to know may be enough to scare them, Julia."

A family with two small children came up to the exhibit, standing next to them. Jack took Julia's hand and said, "We've seen enough here."

"What do you think they'll do, if I just explain to them that all I want to know is who their brother was. That I need to know what kind of kid he was. What games did he like to play? Did he like sports?"

"It's that important to you, huh?"

Julia stopped walking and faced Jack. "What if I write a letter and explain everything to them? What if I just tell them what I told you? I could leave the letter with the secretary at the office."

"I don't know if it's even safe for you to show up there again!" Jack said.

"You could come with me. There's power in numbers."

Jack hesitated, before saying, "That's not a good idea. I mean, it might put them on the defensive to see that someone is with you."

"I'm sorry," Julia said. "I didn't want to get you involved and then I go and make a stupid suggestion."

"No," Jack said, "It's just---"

Julia cut him off. "Well, I'm wasting time going to the zoo and dining at expensive restaurants. Would you mind taking me back to the hotel?"

Jack looked affronted, but agreed. When he pulled up to the hotel, he did a quick reconnaissance with his eyes, before asking, "Did you want to do something for dinner?"

"Depends," Julia said. "We'll see if my letter gets a response."

"I know, I know. They just might change their mind and open up their souls to you."

His tone was sarcastic, but Julia wasn't going to let him deter her. "May I call you later?" she said.

"Sure," Jack replied.

Julia climbed out and waved, but Jack was already on the street driving off. She liked him, but he needed to understand just why she came to Philly. It certainly wasn't to fall in love. She walked into the lobby only to be approached by the woman from the assemblyman's office.

SIX

"Julia!" the woman said, heading her way. She stuck her hand out. "We met yesterday. I'm Mr. Kolson's receptionist, Gail Ryan. Would you mind coming with me?"

"Where?" Julia said with some trepidation.

"We have a private suite. Mr. Kolson is waiting to meet you."

"Here? At the hotel?"

Gail smiled. "Yes. This way you have your privacy."

"Uh, sure," Julia said. "Hold on one minute, please." She went over to the front desk, cutting off a female guest checking in. "Excuse me, this'll only take a minute." She looked over her shoulder to see Gail watching her.

"Ma'am, I'll be with you in a moment," said the desk clerk.

"I'm sorry," she said, "but quickly—see that woman over there?" She tried to be discreet when she pointed, but Gail waved at the clerk.

"Yes, she's with the Kolson party. What could I do for you?"

"Oh, well, I just wanted you to know that she's taking me up to their suite."

"How fortunate for you," said the clerk, his tone oozing with sarcasm.

"You don't understand, I may be in danger. I just wanted someone to see me and know what was going on."

"A regular James Bond situation," said the guest with a laugh and roll of her eye.

With an insolent look, the clerk said, "Will that be all so that I may continue with this transaction?"

"Yes," Julia said, suddenly feeling like a fool. Maybe she was overreacting.

"Everything okay?" Gail asked when she returned to her.

Julia nodded and followed Gail to the elevator, feeling like a sheep being brought to slaughter. They entered the elevator and Julia noticed that Gail pressed floor twenty-three, the top floor.

"Would you mind telling me what this is about?" Julia said.

Gail looked at her curiously. "Well, you should know, you're the one who wanted to see Mr. Kolson, didn't you?"

"Yes, but not necessarily this way. A coffee shop would have been fine."

"Oh, we'll have coffee for you, if you'd like," Gail said as the elevator swept open. Julia followed her down the hallway until Gail stopped and knocked on a door.

Seconds later, a man dressed in slacks and a striped shirt opened the door. He shook her hand, his grip unnecessarily tight. "Julia? I'm Dale Kolson. I understand you want to see me."

Her steps slow and cautious, Julia walked into the suite. It smelled of leather and cologne.

"Thank you, Gail," he said. "That'll be all for now."

Julia turned to watch Gail leave, closing the door behind her.

"Please, come sit," Dale Kolson said. "Would you like something to drink? We have a full bar here and coffee, tea." He led her into a living room.

Julia chose to sit in a chair, as opposed to the couch. "No, thank you. I'm fine."

He sat down across from her. "How is your mother? Ellen, is it?"

Julia's mouth dropped open. "Yes, yes, she's fine."

"Good, good."

"So Gail tells me you have some questions for me."

Julia swallowed hard. "Yes, um, it's about my father, Dennis."

Dale looked to be thinking before he replied. "That's right, you weren't born yet when your father met his misfortune."

"My mother loved him so much and still talks about him to this day, but I wanted to get to know his family and see if they could tell me what kind of boy he was and everything."

Dale Kolson shrugged. "He was the youngest. A bit of a rebel, I'd say. He liked rock and roll and---" He stopped mid-sentence and then said, "Listen, Julia, why don't we cut to the chase here? It's apparent why you're here. How much?"

"What do you mean?"

He chuckled and stood, going over to the bar. "You certainly are a coy one. I suppose we could thank your father for that. How much of the family fortune do you want? My father warned that this day would come even after the tidy sum he sent to your mother."

It was as though she'd been hit with a two by four. She knew nothing of any such exchange of money and said as much to Kolson.

"Well, that's between you and your mother, but didn't you ever wonder how she could afford everything she had?"

"We didn't have a lot, Mr. Kolson." But then again, her mother never worked outside the home and she, Julia, never really wanted for anything. Well, except a father.

"And now you'd like more."

"I don't want a dime. Honestly. All I want is to know more about my father… Dennis."

Kolson studied her. "That's all you want?"

"Yes, and do I have cousins? What are they like?" She paused, and then said, "And I'd like to even know about Katherine."

Kolson stiffened, his face going pale. "How do you know about her?"

Realizing she may have stepped on some sort of landmine, Julia hesitated before explaining. "There was a picture of my father and her. He called her the love of his life."

Kolson leaned in and said sternly, "He was a boy and she was a gold digger. She saw how much money we were worth and planned to get her hands on it. Trying to trick him into marria---"

Suddenly, a man came from another room. "Dale!" he shouted. "That's enough." Julia recognized him as the man from the restaurant the night before. Shaking off his brusqueness, he went over to her and stuck out his hand. "I'm Donald, Dale's brother."

"How do you do?" she said, barely grazing his fingers.

"By the way, thank you for the drinks."

"Sorry?"

"The drinks you bought for my table last night."

She sighed. "Oh, right. Actually, it was my friend who paid for them."

"Friend?"

"Yes, Jack. Jack Landry."

The two men looked at each other. Donald said, "And how do you know this Mr. Landry?"

"Oh, I just met him yesterday." It seemed longer than just a day ago with all that happened.

"Interesting," Dale said. "Why don't you take a word of advice and stay away from your Mr. Landry?"

"This is all making me feel very uncomfortable," Julia said. "I didn't want to start any problems. It's just that I needed to know about my father."

Donald turned to Dale. "I suppose we could have a family reunion. Gather the whole gang. Dad would certainly enjoy that. She could meet all her cousins and..." He started to laugh sarcastically.

"You're making fun of me," Julia said, tears coming to her eyes. "The only pictures I have of him is the wedding photos and the one with....the other one. I'd like to know what medical issues run in the family. And exactly how did my father die? And---"

"Certainly, your mother told you that," Dale said.

"She said it was a hunting accident."

Dale shrugged. "So you do know."

"But there was an investigation. I don't know what happened with that. I don't think my mother knows, either." Then again, she was starting to believe that her mother may have known more than she led Julia to believe.

"He slipped on some ice and the gun went off," Donald said. "It was a tragic accident, nothing more, nothing less."

A tear escaped from Julia's eye, which angered her. She didn't want the two arrogant men seeing her cry. She steeled herself, and said, "Was he like the two of you?"

"In what way?" Dale said.

She wanted to say, cold and dismissive, but instead just shrugged her shoulders.

"Maybe, but we'll never know," Donald said. "You forget that he ran away from home when he was seventeen."

"I knew he left, but didn't know he ran away."

"See, you just learned something new," Donald said.

"Why did he run away?"

"What makes any seventeen-year old run away?" Dale said.

"He was heartbroken. The love of his life died!"

"The love of his life?" Dale said.

She knew it was risky, but she blurted, "Katherine."

"I think we're about done here," Donald said. "We told you all we know."

Dale stood, indicating the door. "I'll see you out."

Julia got up. "Please, just if you find any pictures of him or anything else that would acquaint me with my father, would you please send them to me?"

"Absolutely!" Dale replied.

"Let me give you my address." Julie reached into her purse for her notepad.

"That's not necessary. We already have it."

"What?" Julia asked.

"You think we first don't do a background check on anyone who tries to contact us on personal matters?" Donald said.

"It's the life of a politician," Dale added, opening the door.

Julia walked out, feeling shell shocked and even more frustrated than when she first arrived in Philly. Gail was nowhere around as far as Julia could tell.

She went to her room several floors below and, even though it was only about five in the evening, she cried herself to sleep.

An hour later, she woke up and realized she needed to call Jack right away. When he answered on the first ring she asked if she could take him out to dinner.

"So no word, huh?"

"Actually, quite the opposite," she said. ""How about we meet at the pub? I can be there in about fifteen minutes."

"You're a brave woman to want to go back there with the way Ron treated you," Jack said.

"Well, it was cheap and the food, from what I had of it, was good."

"Okay, give me a half hour and I'll be there."

SEVEN

Julia got to the pub before Jack and asked for a quiet table, even though it was apparent the moment she walked in it would be difficult to find any quiet nook or corner. Unlike the first time when she ate at the near-empty establishment, this time the bar was jammed with raucous patrons shouting to be heard.

She tried to see if Ron was behind the bar, but it was too crowded.

"Follow me," the hostess yelled to Julia, bringing her all the way to the back to a table for two, which was next to a larger table filled with a group of celebratory girls. It wasn't quite as noisy as it was at the bar, but didn't offer much in the way of privacy.

"I'm meeting a friend here," Julia called to the hostess. "I hope he's able to find me."

"He by himself?"

"Yes."

"Okay, I'll be on the lookout. Your waitress will be over in a few."

Julia surreptitiously glanced at the girls celebrating. One young woman had on a crown and a sash with the words Bride-to-Be scrolled across it. "To Katie!" the girls shouted, all taking one shot after the next.

It was so much different from Julia's bachelorette party, if one could call it that.

Her mother took her out to a quiet dinner and presented her with a check for ten thousand dollars as a pre-wedding gift. She'd been stunned at the time, not to mention confused.

How could her mother afford to write such an expensive check? But she had and it didn't bounce. She also helped pay for the wedding, even though Julia and Kevin tried to keep it small. It had been intimate but sweet.

So had been the marriage—for the first couple of years. She wondered if she'd ever find love again, and at that very thought, Jack appeared.

"Hey!" he shouted, pulling out the wooden chair across from her.

"I didn't realize it was going to be like this here," she said.

"I should've warned you."

Just then the celebratory table broke out into song: "Goin' to the chapel and you're goin' to get married..."

Their waitress swung by and dropped a couple of menus at the table before disappearing into the crowd. Jack shifted his chair closer to Julia's. "We'll make it work," he said. "Besides, it's a good excuse to get closer to you."

In spite of herself, Julia couldn't help but smile, which instigated a kiss from Jack full on the lips. The girls at the next table started with wolf whistles, encouraging him to continue. Jack laughed, but did no such thing.

"So, tell me," he said, leaning into Julia, "what happened?"

Julia started to tell him when the waitress returned to take their order. "Oh," Julia said, "I haven't even looked at the menu, yet."

"I'll take the ribs, fries and a side of slaw," Jack said without having glimpsed the menu.

"And a Guinness?" the waitress said.

Jack concurred with a nod.

"Same here," Julia shouted.

"Guinness, too?" the waitress said.

"Sure," Julia said. She'd never had the dark ale before, but was willing to try it. The waitress took off to put in their orders.

"Well," Julia said, "you'll never believe the afternoon I had."

Jack focused solely on her as if the bar wasn't filled with activity and merriment. "I'm all ears," he said.

Julia began, telling him everything that transpired, how she was escorted up to the suite, how they frustrated her by not giving her much information. "Except, I now know that my mom wasn't being totally upfront with me. She knows more than she's telling me."

"Did you call her?"

"No, I need to confront her face to face." Julia picked up her glass of beer and took a sip. She made a face.

"No?" Jack said.

She shook her head. "Think I'll stick to the water." She slid her beer closer to him.

The table next to them paid the bill and brought the party over to the bar, which helped the noise level in the corner.

Soon, their meals were delivered with far less presentation than the night before, but neither seemed to care. Instead, Jack and Julia ate while trying to figure out exactly what happened with her father.

"I'll tell you one thing," she said, "they looked disturbed when I mentioned Katherine."

Jack stopped chewing. "Katherine?"

Julia nodded. "Yeah, apparently my father was quite a bit younger, but head over heels in love with her. I didn't think it was a big deal, but when I mentioned her, Dale got angry. He tried to hide it. Called her a gold digger."

Jack took in a deep breath, and muttered, "Those sons of bitches."

"I don't know, Jack, I think maybe my mother needs to fill in the pieces since it seems the Kolsons aren't going to be much more help."

"When are you thinking about going back home?"

"Tomorrow. First thing in the morning."

Jack cleared his throat. "Think I could join you?" Before he gave her a chance to answer, he leaned in and kissed her.

Julia wanted more than just a kiss, but she also wasn't sure if it was a good idea she bring him with her to confront her mother. She said as much.

"I wouldn't be intrusive, babe."

"I do like being with you," Julia said, enjoying that he so casually called her "babe."

They'd finished their meals and while Jack polished off the two glasses of beer, he began to caress her leg with his free hand. When the bill came, he snagged it and said he wasn't going to let her pay.

"But that's not fair. I said I would take you out."

"No lady of mine is going to pay for me." He kissed her again.

Once the bill was taken care of and the tip on the table, he took her hand, walking her back to the hotel, explaining that his vehicle was parked nearby.

While standing outside, he whispered in her ear, "I wouldn't say no, if you invited me to your room?"

"You're invited," she said, feeling something she hadn't felt in quite some time.

***

Later, their naked bodies entwined around each other, Julia couldn't believe how happy she was. Earlier, she'd wondered if she'd ever fall in love again, but then only a few hours later, exhausted and spent from the lovemaking, she accepted the possibility.

Jack played with her hair, lifting her blonde tendrils and bringing them to his face. He said, "You've had quite a couple days of adventure, I'd say."

"I did," she agreed. "I wasn't sure I was going to survive the face to face with your assemblyman."

"Dale Kolson is not my assemblyman!" he said.

Julia laughed. "Well, it seems he doesn't care too much for you either."

Jack pushed her off him. He sat up, glaring at her. "What do you mean, Julia?"

She stared at him, wondering why the sudden change in attitude. "I just mentioned that you were a friend I'd made while here and they asked me about it."

"What'd they ask?"

"Just how did I know you?"

"Shit!" Jack said, jumping out of bed.

"Jack, what is going on?" Julia said, wrapping a sheet around herself.

"I have to go."

"Why? What did I say?"

"Listen, I can't be seen with you." Jack slipped on his pants, shirt and shoes in record time.

"You are more connected to all this than you told me, aren't you?"

"I'll call you in a couple of days," he said, rushing out the door without kissing her goodbye.

EIGHT

The following day, after leaving a couple of messages for Jack without him picking up, Julia checked out of the hotel, got her car and headed back to Long Island.

Instead of blasting music for company, she kept trying to figure out what had Jack in such a panicked state. That's when it occurred to her that maybe it had something to do with him being a reporter.

But why run away? Then her insecurities got a hold of her and she wondered if maybe his reaction was all an act, maybe he just wanted to use her and then find an excuse to leave her just like that.

She pounded her steering wheel, chastising herself for giving in to his advances. It had been delightful, but it was a good reminder that someone always got hurt when emotions came into play, and she seemed to always be that someone.

Instead of going to her new apartment, she drove directly to her mother's. She was worn out, but didn't want to wait a second more to get more information that she was sure her mother had.

She went up to the door and rang the bell. Moments later, her mother answered. Julia could tell by Ellen's apprehensive expression that she was dreading this visit.

"We need to talk," Julia said, walking in and heading to the living room.

Ellen followed behind. "What...what did you find out?"

"You tell me, Mom. What do you think I found out?"

Ellen sat down across from her daughter. She looked to be drained of blood. "Any number of things, I suppose."

"I am an idiot," Julia said. "I can't trust anyone, not even my own mother!"

"Don't say that, honey. Please don't," Ellen said, her bottom lip quivering.

"They asked how you were; they knew your name, Mom! They said they gave you money. Money for what?"

Ellen sucked up some air. "Goodness. Besides a life insurance policy that your father had, his grandfather had left him a nice amount in his will, which was to go to his closest family member upon his death. They knew I was pregnant with you and I guess they wanted to do the right thing."

"The right thing? They had no interest in seeing their niece, but would rather just send money?"

"I'm sure you found out just how...influential the Kolsons are."

"What do you mean, Mom?"

Ellen stared off into space, her voice going soft, almost mechanical. "When you're young and feel you have so much to lose, you play their game."

"Mom, what are you saying?"

"Your father did go to see them all those years ago, but I didn't want him to. He wasn't right—mentally. Not after I told him I was pregnant. He started talking more and more about Katherine. I didn't know what to make of it."

Julia watched as her mother seemed to go back in time.

"See, he always suspected that Katherine, the love of his life, was murdered. He said her car going off that bridge the way it did was suspicious. His father---"

"David?"

Ellen looked up at Julia and nodded. "Yes, David. He was against the relationship. Katherine was quite a bit older than your father and when she told him she was pregnant, well, David hit the roof. He was a powerful man and, apparently, this woman not only was considered undesirable, but her presence would hinder his ambitions."

"What kind of ambitions?" Julia said.

"Political."

"Apparently, David threatened Katherine, reminding her she had relations with an under-aged boy, even though he was almost eighteen."

"Do you think she was trying to trick him into marrying her?"

Ellen shrugged. "Who knows. The dead tell no tales."

"But they could've had her arrested for being with a minor. It doesn't make sense."

"Not to us, but when your father went back to Philadelphia, it was to confront his father about Katherine's death. He'd never stopped loving her. I found that out too late."

"And?"

"He threatened him, and his brothers, that he was going to go to the police, ask them to open up the investigation."

"How do you know all this, Mom?"

"He called me before he went to confront them. He was upset. He said that his brothers had been taunting him, telling him that pregnant women can't drive straight and veer off bridges all the time."

Tears were streaming down her mother's cheeks. "I begged him not to go. I just had a bad feeling about it."

"They killed Dad, didn't they?" Julia's mouth was dry, her heart pounding.

Her voice tight, Ellen said, "That is never a discussion we can have. Never."

"Mom?" Julia said, staring at a woman who was suddenly a stranger to her.

"Your father never really wanted me. You see things much clearer over time. I was only a substitute for his passion, but I got what I wanted," Ellen said. "I was going to have a baby. Surely, you of all people can understand that desire, Julia."

"You didn't go to the police, tell them what you suspected?" Julia cried.

"Why? Why should I when your father loved Katherine? Katherine Landry, the love of his life."

"Landry?" Julia gasped.

EPISODE 2

ONE

Exhausted and in a state of shock, Julia wandered into her apartment.

She'd only rented it a few weeks earlier after having sold her house. She hadn't even unpacked anything other than the essentials before she'd dashed off to Philadelphia in search of information; therefore, the space was unfamiliar and cold to her, boxes yet to be emptied.

Landry. Jack's last name was Landry. The same as Katherine's. It couldn't have been a coincidence, could it? Had he used her somehow for his own gain?

She tossed her purse on a stack of boxes and dropped down onto her couch. Just then the muffled sound of her cell phone ringing came from her purse. She jumped up to grab it, scrambling to find the phone, hoping it was Jack.

She pulled it out only to see that it was Kevin's number. What could her ex possibly want? The marriage was over. The divorce papers signed.

"Hello," she said.

"Hey, how's it going?" Kevin said.

She wasn't going to tell him the truth so just said, "Fine."

"I, uh," he said, "I just wanted to be the one to let you know before anyone else told you."

Any more bad news and she was sure she'd have a breakdown. "Tell me what?" she said with hesitation.

"Stacy and I are getting married this weekend."

Married? So soon? "Okay," she said, her throat closing up.

"I'm sorry, Julia, it's just---"

"I get it, Kevin. I hope you and Stacy have lots of children." She hung up.

Nothing in her life was what she'd thought it was. Her ex was getting married, even though he'd promised her he'd love her in sickness and in health. She supposed that infertility didn't fit in between those two parameters.

Her mother knew much more about Julia's father than she ever let on, and maybe sold out by not reporting what she'd suspected. Murder? How could her mother let her own husband go to his grave the way he did as a victim?

And then there was Jack. How innocent he'd been pretending to care, to make love to her as though he had meant it.

She was tired of being a casualty on so many fronts and decided she needed to let Jack know that she was on to him.

She hit redial since his number had been the last one she'd called. He hadn't picked up before and she doubted he would do so this time.

Instead of apologizing while begging for an explanation, her message would be much different from her previous ones. She waited for his voicemail.

"Hello."

"Jack?" she said, surprised he'd answered.

"Listen, I'm sorry about how I left you. I know it seems strange to you, but you don't understand---"

"Oh, but I do," she said. "Jack Landry. When were you going to tell me that you're related to Katherine?"

There was silence for a moment before he replied, "Okay, okay, we need to talk. I'm coming to see you tomorrow."

"I don't know if I want to see you," she said. And, yet, there was part of her that did.

"I can explain myself...please."

After weighing it over, Julia agreed and gave him her address. "I'll be there around noon time," he said before hanging up.

Julia looked around her apartment, realizing she had to give it some sense of order and spent the next few hours emptying the rest of her boxes, putting dishes into cabinets, towels and sheets in the hall closet.

She then realized how hungry she was and ordered Chinese. After eating Lo Mein and Sesame Chicken, she headed to bed.

However, she couldn't sleep, her mind going over how she'd walked out on her mother, telling her she didn't know who she was.

"Julia!" Ellen had cried, "You don't understand. I was in a difficult situation."

"You're right, Mom," she said. "I don't understand." She slammed the front door and left.

As far as she could recall, that was the first time she and her mother had a falling out. She wasn't sure anything could mend their relationship. This was just too big.

TWO

Sure enough, right around noon the next day her doorbell rang. She opened it just a crack to confirm it was her expected company. It was.

She let Jack in, but backed away so he wouldn't expect a kiss. His eyes were strained, his clothes disheveled, and he looked like he had a five o'clock shadow.

"Who's Katherine?" Julia said, without inviting him to sit down.

He sighed and seemed to be looking beyond the living room. "Before we get into all that, could I use your bathroom first? I didn't make any stops."

Julia pointed down the hall. "It's the second door on the right."

"And, would it be too much trouble for a cup of coffee?" he said, heading to the bathroom.

"You've got balls," Julia said. Even so, she went into the kitchen to put on a pot.

When she heard the bathroom door open, she called, "I'm in here."

Jack walked in, watching her turn on the coffee pot and pull some mugs from her cabinet. "I take it black," he said.

"Good, because I don't have any milk right now. I actually don't have much in the way of food. I haven't been here that long."

"Julia," he said, "you have to know that it was dumb luck that our paths crossed when you came to Philly. Even if you hadn't mentioned the Kolson name, I would've tried to get to know you."

"I find that hard to believe."

"Trust me," Jack said. "So do I. I mean, I wasn't in the market to meet anyone and I did wonder if maybe you were someone who was investigating those crooks and made up that story about Dennis being your dad. I admit, I was intrigued."

"Intrigued, how?" she said, pouring him his coffee, and setting it in front of him.

"Well, you're very pretty and sweet. It wasn't long before I realized that you were innocent in what you wanted to know about your father, but then when you got that threatening phone call, it confirmed to me that the Kolsons are guilty of something."

"But why did you run when I told you that they knew you and I were friends?"

Jack cleared his throat. "Katherine was my aunt, my dad's sister."

Julia scowled. "Your aunt?"

"Yeah, I was just a kid when she was murdered."

"Are you sure she was murdered? Couldn't it have been an accident?"

"Yeah, just like your father's death was an accident." Jack took a sip of his coffee. "Here's the thing," he said, "our family wasn't too pleased that she was seeing a Kolson. The Landry clan didn't ever get along with the Kolsons and Aunt Katherine knew that, but she was in a fight with her parents—my grandparents—so she took advantage of a young guy who was smitten by her good looks and charm. To piss my grandparents off."

"So she didn't love my dad?"

Jack shrugged. "I can't answer that."

"But she was going to have his baby."

"The autopsy report never mentioned her being pregnant. We think she was lying about that."

Julia couldn't help but dislike this woman that she'd been feeling pity for up till now. "None of this makes sense."

"It sure is complicated," Jack said. "All I know is that my father wants the Kolsons to pay for his sister's death and he said he'll never give up."

"Well, all I know is that my father loved her, even after he married my mom."

Jack put down his cup. "What do you mean?"

"I went to my mother's yesterday. She did know more. Just like you, she thinks they killed my dad."

"Hmm, think she'd talk to me about it?"

"Are you investigating this?" Julia said.

"Well, let's just say it is one reason why I chose the career path I did. My dad, her brother, has been eaten up by this for years."

"I wouldn't count on my mom helping, though, Jack. She said she'd never talk about it again."

"Unless she's subpoenaed."

Julia stared at him. "Don't you have to have some kind of evidence for that?"

"That's what I've been working on for as long as I remember. What's interesting is that rumor had it for years that your father committed suicide. According to the police reports that I could find on record, your father had been away for years, but came back to Philadelphia to take his own life on Kolson property. As some sort of punishment to them. The Kolsons played it up that they wanted their privacy in such a delicate matter, but my father didn't believe them."

"Why?"

"Well, my dad told me that Dennis, your dad, went to see him just before the so-called suicide. He said that Dennis was upset. Mind you, my dad didn't think very highly of your father so he didn't want to hear what he had to say, but when he was told that my aunt may have been forced off the bridge by the Kolsons, it confirmed his own suspicions."

"Still, Jack," Julia said, "people do get in car accidents sometimes."

"It was a clear summer night, Julia. The car was impounded and there was no mechanical failure."

"Maybe she was upset. Maybe she lost control because of--"

"No, I don't think so. This stinks to high heaven." He polished off his coffee. "Julia, seriously, I'm sorry about the way I reacted after...you know, we made love."

"I don't know why you felt you had to leave like that. In such a rush. You know, it can make a girl feel paranoid."

He reached over, resting his hand on hers. "I'm sorry. Really. And it could've been a bit of an overreaction, I admit, but the Kolsons know that I've been on their tail for a couple of years now and they've made some not-so-subtle warnings in an attempt to get me to stop."

"What kind of threats?"

He shrugged. "Similar to your phone call. I have to be careful. They can't know that I haven't given up."

"Oh, Jack, I wish you would've told me. I never would've mentioned your name to them."

"It never occurred to me that you would. Guess that was lame on my part."

"So did you get another call," Julia said, "threatening you?"

"No," Jack said. "Not directly, anyway, but I did get a phone call from the paper that sends me out on assignments, telling me they won't be able to give me any more work. They don't have the budget for it."

"Couldn't that be a coincidence?" Julia said.

"Sure, but I doubt it. The Kolsons buy a lot of advertising for that paper. If it weren't for them, quite likely the paper wouldn't be in business."

"Doesn't your boss know that you have been investigating the Kolsons all this time?"

"On my dime, Julia. This is a story I'm working on for my dad...and my aunt. May she rest in peace."

Julia pointed to his empty cup. "Care for another?" she said.

Jack shook his head, taking a deep breath. "Listen, I need to get a room somewhere and settle in for a few days."

"A few days? Won't that hinder the investigation?"

"Oh, babe, I got to lay low for a while."

Jack calling her babe reminded her of their time together in Philly before he took off.

Now that she knew why, though, she forgave him. She said, "You know, you don't really need to get a room." She actually smiled, which surprised her.

Raising an eyebrow, he said, "You sure?"

She nodded. "As a matter of fact, I don't think either of us got much sleep lately. Maybe an afternoon nap would be what we need."

Jack stood, taking her hand. "Lead the way, babe."

***

Later, Julia woke up in Jack's arms. He was snoring lightly. She played with the hair on his chest, quietly savoring the afternoon of tender kisses mixed with intense fervor. After, they both fell asleep.

Now that she was awake, she started to think about all that he'd told her. She was tempted to just forget about her father, Katherine and the Kolsons and start her new life—just like Kevin was doing. She couldn't believe he was going to get married so quickly after their divorce.

And then there was her mother. She didn't know what to make of that, especially since her mother hadn't called her since she'd walked out in a huff. Her mother always called her everyday—sometimes twice in one day.

She looked up to see that Jack's eyes were open and he was watching her. "Did you have a good rest?" she said.

"Sure did." He kissed her on the forehead.

"You must be hungry," she said.

"You could say that."

"I have to get groceries anyway. Why don't I run to the store and you settle in, take a shower, if you want."

"You sure you don't want me to go with you?"

"Only if you want to," she said.

"Not necessarily, but is it possible to pick up something that we could make here? I don't feel like going out tonight."

"No problem," she said. "I'd let you use my computer or watch some television, but I haven't hooked anything up, yet."

"That's okay. I think I will take advantage of your shower and give myself a shave." He rubbed his scruffy face. "Sorry if it was rough on you, even though you didn't seem to mind."

Julia laughed. "No, but I do like you clean shaven." She climbed out of bed and started to dress. "I shouldn't be too long. Make yourself at home."

THREE

The grocery store was only a half mile from the apartment, but different from the one she used to go to near the house she'd sold. She had to familiarize herself with its layout, which frustrated her since she wanted to get in and out as quickly as possible.

She pushed the cart up and down each aisle, tossing a box of pasta in, some fresh vegetables, and a whole chicken. She tried to remember what was in her cabinets, food wise—not much.

She went down the beverage aisle and realized Jack would appreciate a cold beer or two and picked up a six-pack of his favorite.

"Never would've picked you for a Guinness fan."

Julia looked up to see a man wearing sunglasses, t-shirt and jeans standing next to her. "Oh, it's not for me."

The man scowled. "Damn. So you're not single?"

Julia wasn't used to being hit on; then again, it hadn't been that long since she'd stopped wearing her wedding band.

Yet, she didn't know how to answer the question so just ignored the man and walked away wishing she'd made a grocery list before leaving the apartment.

Satisfied that she had all she would need for at least a couple of days sustenance, she went to the register to be rung up.

She hadn't made a nice meal in ages. It was just herself and she'd usually pick on a salad or make a sandwich. It was exciting to think she'd be preparing dinner for someone else.

She got to the car, unlocked the trunk and loaded up the few bags. When she went to open the door to the driver's side, she looked up to see the man who'd hit on her earlier standing there. She jumped from surprise.

"Do me a favor, would ya," he said. "Give your boyfriend my regards."

Shaking, Julia hurriedly jumped inside her car and immediately locked the door.

Granted, the neighborhood she moved into wasn't quite as nice as what she had been used to, but this guy was brazen and intimidating.

She refused to look at him while she started her car and backed out of the parking spot.

She did watch, though, to be sure he wasn't following her. As far as she could tell, he wasn't and when she got to her apartment, she pulled into her designated spot.

She spotted Jack standing in the walkway, his hands in his pockets.

"Hey," he said. "I was starting to worry about you." He came over as she popped the trunk. He grabbed three of the four bags.

"I haven't gotten used to this area, yet, which is why it took me so long." She looked around the parking lot. "By the way, where's your vehicle?"

"A few blocks from here," he said. He leaned in. "You okay?"

"Why, do I seem frazzled?"

He nodded.

"Let's go inside," she said, grabbing the remaining bag.

She made sure her car was locked and followed Jack up the steps and into the apartment.

When she walked in, she saw that her computer was set up on the desk in the corner, just where she'd planned to put it anyway, and the TV was on. "Oh, my goodness," she said, "you've been busy."

"Hope you don't mind," he said, carrying the bags to the kitchen.

"Not at all! This is great. Thank you so much." She placed her grocery bag and purse on the table and went up to Jack, wrapping her arms around him. "I could get used to this."

"I was going to hang those up for you," he said, pointing to the stack of pictures leaning against the wall, "but figured you'd have specific places you'd want them."

"I hadn't really thought much about any of that," she said.

"So, what happened? Why are you upset?"

"Just some creep was hitting on me," she said.

"You should be used to that."

"I'm not. You're the first one I've been with since my divorce. Besides, there was something particularly creepy about him. He said to say hello to my boyfriend."

Jack scowled. "Your boyfriend?"

"I may have implied I had a boyfriend in the store when he noticed I was buying Guinness. Just to get him to back off."

"You bought me Guinness?"

She nodded. "He said something like he didn't think I'd be a fan of that kind of beer, so I said---" She stopped herself. "Wait, I didn't say anything. I just walked away without acknowledging him."

"So, when did he say something about your boyfriend?"

"When I went to load the groceries in my car. He was standing right next to it, staring at me."

"What'd he look like?"

"I told you, creepy."

"I need more description than that," Jack said, walking over to the window. He surreptitiously pulled back the curtain and surveyed the outside. "And I wonder how he knew which car was yours."

"Wait," Julia said, "do you think he is one of Kolson's people?"

Jack looked over his shoulder at her. "I wouldn't be surprised. So...?"

"I don't know. He was about six feet tall, a little chunky. He had on a white t-shirt and some jeans. I took him to be a construction worker or something."

"Did you see what he was driving?" He dropped the curtain back into place and headed toward the kitchen.

"No, but I kept looking to see if I was being followed and I don't think I was." She sighed in exasperation, her voice quivering. "Oh, Jack, I can't live like this, always wondering if we're being followed and threatened. Somehow this has got to stop."

"Well, I'm already in too deep, babe. If you want to stay out of it, that's fine. Maybe I should put myself up in a hotel anyway."

"Why?" she said.

"Well, I don't want you to be in any danger."

"Is that why you parked a few blocks away?"

He shrugged as if to say, perhaps.

She didn't want Jack to leave. His company was welcoming. "Can we just forget about it for now and assume the guy was just hitting on me?" Julia started unpacking the groceries. "I'll make dinner and you have a beer or two."

"I could go for a cold one," Jack said, pulling the six-pack out of a bag. "Would you happen to have a bottle opener?"

Julia scowled. "Hmm, it's not a twist top?" she said, going to her utensil drawer, pushing around forks, knives and spoons in search of a bottle opener. "Oh, gosh," she said. "I could go out and buy one."

"No problem," Jack said, taking the bottle over to her counter. While holding it with a tight grip and resting the bottle against the edge, he used his other hand and smacked down. "Voila!" he said, the cap popping off.

"Oh my gosh," Julia said. "I've never seen that before. Kevin, my ex, rarely drank beer."

All of a sudden, she started to think of Kevin as somewhat ineffectual. He wasn't handy around the house and wouldn't know how to open a beer the way Jack just did if his life depended on it.

Jack on the other hand seemed to have smart sense. And she liked the way the muscles in his arms flexed when he open the beer in a matter of seconds.

"Could I help with dinner?" Jack said.

"No, that's okay. Why don't you kick back and watch some TV. Everything should be ready in a little over an hour."

FOUR

"You're a good cook," Jack said, pushing his cleaned plate away from him, and patting his stomach with satisfaction.

"I learned from my mom," Julia said. "She loved to make big meals even if it was just for the two of us."

"Does she have a large family on her side?"

"Not really," Julia said. "She has an older sister, but she lives in California. My grandparents, her parents, both died a few years ago, within weeks of each other."

"Julia, I really would like to meet her."

Julia didn't say anything right away. She knew her mother would clam up once she found out that Jack was stirring up the past. She said, "How about I introduce you as a guy I'm seeing? We won't say how we know each other. I won't even tell her you're from Philly."

"What will that gain me?" Jack said.

"Time…until we can try to get her to open up."

Jack collected their dirty plates and brought them to the dishwasher.

"I can get those, Jack," Julia said, jumping up. "You enjoy your beer." She nudged him back to the table and began loading the dishwasher.

Then something occurred to her.

She said, "Wait, I have something to show you."

She ran down the hallway and opened the hall closet. On the top shelf was the box filled with her father's things, including the photo of Katherine.

She brought it into the kitchen and set it in front of Jack, who was sipping on his third beer.

"What's this?" he said.

"Stuff from my dad." Her mother never asked for the box back and Julia had packed it with her stuff when she had moved.

He gazed up at her. "Okay if I go through it?"

"Yeah, I don't think there's much really that will reveal anything, but you're the detective, maybe you'll see something that could lead to something."

"Not a detective," Jack said, opening the box. "A reporter who's investigating on his own time, which it seems I'll be having quite a lot of now that the paper has decided to cut me off."

Julia went back to putting leftovers away and cleaning up; every once in awhile she looked at him to check his expression, which didn't divulge much.

Once she was finished, she went over and sat down. He had the Boy Scout badges and sea shell on the table in front of him, the photo in his hand.

"She really was a looker," he said. "That sounds disturbing, my being her nephew and all."

Julia gave him a sad smile. "I'm sorry. This must be rough on you."

"You know, sometimes I wonder if I would keep this up, if my father was no longer around."

"You never told me just what set your father off from liking the Kolsons—I mean before everything. What started the feud?"

"Feud? I wouldn't really call it a feud. We're not the Hatfields and McCoys."

"So, what started it?"

Jack tossed the picture on the table. "They were competing against each other in the booming housing industry. Only problem is David Kolson had the money to buy off the politicians to make sure Kolson Construction got most of the work. Have to say, his timing with buying and selling is impressive. My father wasn't able to grow his business the way he wanted to, since the Kolsons were in collusion with the powers that be."

He looked at Julia. "Doesn't seem like much, does it? Maybe my dad is coming off as petty, but something like that can fester—especially when you see things are so shady."

He reached back into the box while he continued to talk. "You know, I think it was just too much for my father with how much he wanted to succeed and saw those sons of bitches as a big hindrance, so he decided to be up the Kolsons' asses as much as he could. He even tried to run for public office to get them out, but they just had way too much money to compete with and Dad didn't even come close to winning. He took that pretty hard, too."

Jack reached into the box, feeling around. He pulled out the key.

"I wonder why he'd kept that," Julia said.

Jack studied it. "It's a car key."

"Really? How can you tell?"

"It has the words 'Nissan Motor' on it."

"Oh, I never even noticed that," Julia said.

"My aunt drove a Datsun pickup."

"Oh, well, I guess then it wouldn't be---"

"Nissan made Datsuns," he said, his jaw tightening.

Julia gazed at him, knowing he was on to something.

"Okay, I'll play your game," Jack said, as if resigned.

"What game?"

"Introduce me to your mother. Tell her we're dating. It's not a lie."

"But how will that get you what you need to know?"

"I don't know, yet, but I'll figure it out."

Julia knew then that she'd have to call her mother, tell her she was sorry for how she'd treated her and ask if she and Jack could come over the next day. "All right," she said. She got up and went to get her cell phone.

Ellen answered; her tone hesitant. Julia did apologize, as difficult as it was, and then mentioned that she'd met a guy. "I'd like you to meet him, Mom."

Her mother's voice suddenly sounded lighthearted. "That would be lovely, honey. When were you thinking?"

Julia looked over at Jack and mouthed, "When?"

"Any time," he said in a whisper.

"How about tomorrow morning? We'll bring donuts, if you have coffee on."

"Wonderful! I am looking forward to meeting him. What's his name?"

Something told Julia to lie. She said, "Bill. Bill Datsun."

FIVE

The following morning, Jack and Julia were sitting with Julia's mother at the dining room table.

Ellen had put out her good china and made a crumb cake fresh out of the oven, even though Julia had told her they'd be bringing doughnuts, which no one touched while the crumb cake was close to being polished off.

"This is the best crumb cake I've had in ages," Jack, who was now being referred to as Bill, said.

Ellen waved him off. "Julia is a great cook, too. I enjoy her chocolate fudge cake. She makes it for my birthday every year."

"You have a nice place here, Mrs. Kolson," Jack said. "You been here long?"

"Oh, several years," Ellen said. "And what do you do, Bill, for a living that is?"

Julia jumped into the conversation. "He teaches, Mom. It's how I met him."

"Oh? I don't remember you mentioning him," Ellen said.

"Well, I wasn't ready to date then."

"Would you mind if I use your bathroom?" Jack said.

"Not at all," Ellen said. "It's down the hall, first door on the left."

The moment he was out of earshot, Ellen looked over at Julia and said, "He seems very nice. When did you start seeing him?"

Julia hesitated, and then said, "Uh, a few weeks ago."

"And you said nothing to me?"

"I wasn't sure about him, yet."

Jack came back, but didn't come into the dining room. Instead, he stood in the living room, which was right off the dining room, looking around, as if admiring it.

He walked over to a painting hanging on the wall. It was of a forest with a river cutting through it "Where's this painted?" he said.

"Oh, I don't even know," Ellen said. "It's certainly not anything expensive."

Jack shifted, as if looking at other knickknacks scattered around the living room. "Is this you, sweetie?" he said, pointing to a photo of Julia.

"Oh, gosh," Julia said. "That was taken on my first day of kindergarten."

"I have a picture of her first day of school all the way through to her senior year," Ellen said.

"She sure does," Julia said. "Much to my embarrassment."

Jack laughed, and then shifted to the wedding photo of Julia's parents. Julia felt her stomach tighten, knowing this was how Jack was going to start his interrogation.

Feigning surprise, he said, "This isn't you, Mrs. Kolson, is it?"

"It is," Ellen said.

Jack picked up the photo. "You still have the same deep blue eyes. Your husband was one lucky fella."

Julia could barely breathe while her mother cleared her throat, and then said, "I don't know about that. It wasn't long after that picture was taken that he died."

Jack put the photo down. "I'm so sorry to hear that." He came back into the dining room and sat down. "Would you mind telling me how? I don't mean to be nosy, but---" He left the "but" hanging there as if in anticipation.

"I'm sure Julia could fill you in, Bill." Ellen's bottom lip began to quiver and tears came to her eyes. "She seems to have more information about everything now."

"Mrs. Kolson," he started to say, "I'd like--"

"Jack, please don't!" Julia interrupted.

Ellen looked from Julia to Jack. She said, "Jack? I thought you said your name was Bill."

"Mom," Julia said, "I'm sorry. This is Jack---" She started to say his last name, but knew that would just put her mother over the edge.

"Mrs. Kolson," he said, "I am dating your daughter, yes. But I'm not a teacher. I'm a reporter. I've been hired to investigate the Kolsons. They have had some shady dealings and---"

Ellen scrambled to get up out her chair. "Get out, get out now! The two of you!"

"Mom, please don't." Julia reached over, pulling her mother back down in her chair. "I never knew that my needing to know about dad would lead to this mess. I am not going to judge you, but I know too much now. I'm not that little girl in kindergarten any longer. I can handle whatever you have to tell me."

Ellen glared at Jack. "This all happened years ago. Why are you doing this now? It's over. People have died, others have had to live with it."

"True," Jack said, "but...but I'm trying to get some closure for my father."

Ellen studied Jack dubiously. "Your father, why?"

Julia didn't bother trying to stop Jack. She knew that he needed to jump in with both feet in order to provide an adequate explanation.

"Mrs. Kolson, Katherine Landry was my aunt, my father's sister."

The blood drained from Ellen's face.

"If you know anything, anything at all that could help me get some answers, I would be so grateful."

"Grateful?" Ellen said, her voice shaky. "You want me to break a promise so that you can feel grateful?"

Julia shifted her chair closer to her mother. "What promise, Mom? What did you have to promise?"

Ellen bit her lip, tears streaming down her face. "I wasn't that way, ever. I was a nice person, Julia. You have to believe me."

"We aren't questioning that," Jack said.

"He needed me. I was his saving grace."

"Who, Dad?" Julia said.

Ellen looked down, playing with the wedding band on her finger. She'd never stopped wearing it.

"I fell in love with him. Julia, you have to know that. I loved your father when I married him.

"He didn't feel the same way about you, did he, Mrs. Kolson?" Jack's tone was gentle.

She shook her head. "It wasn't long after we were married that I found that out. He kept comparing me to that older woman, the love of his life. Every day it seems he got worse and worse. He wasn't right, in the head. I found it difficult to live with him."

"Did he hit you, Mom?" Julia said.

Ellen shrugged, dismissing the question. "One day he just took off and didn't come back. I was all alone."

"But then he called you, Mom. He told you that Dale and Donald basically admitted to killing Katherine."

"I told you that?" Ellen said, her eyes widening.

"Yes, right after I came back from Philly."

"I shouldn't have said anything. I shouldn't be talking now."

"You promised the Kolsons you wouldn't say what you knew, didn't you?"

"I'm not a bad person. I was scared. I was alone. I had no idea how I was going to bring a baby into this world by myself. And properly care for her."

"So they paid you to keep quiet."

"I didn't get rich or anything," she said. "I got enough to provide for my daughter and me. And they never admitted to me that they killed anybody. You must know that. They said that Dennis committed suicide."

"So, the hunting accident...," Julia said.

"It's the story I had to tell you. I didn't want you to think your father would do something so horrible."

"But he didn't, Mom!" Julia shouted. "They killed him when he threatened to go to the police."

Ellen scowled, looking confused. "That's right. I have been able to put that out of my mind all these years, until--"

"Until I went looking to find out about my father," Julia said.

"Mrs. Kolson, I need to get a statement from you. Would you be willing to do that?"

Julia watched her mother closely. She appeared to have shrunk, her very spirit collapsing.

"Mom?" Julia said. "These people have to be stopped."

"I'm so tired," Ellen said breathlessly.

"I know," Julia said, putting her hand on her mother's. "But would you be willing to give a statement?"

"What kind of statement?"

"What you just told me," Jack said. "Would you be willing to tell the police?"

"I...I have to think about it," Ellen said. "Please, just let me rest awhile."

Jack didn't say anything right away, but then agreed. Then to Julia, he added, "Why don't we give her some time and then come back later."

Julia nodded. "Mom, you go rest. We'll be back this afternoon."

"The crumb cake was delicious, Mrs. Kolson," Jack said, pushing out his chair and standing. "I hope Julia has the recipe."

Ellen forced a smile and walked them to the door. "Oh, did you want to take the doughnuts? I won't be able to eat all those."

"We'll have them this afternoon, when we come back," Julia said.

Ellen grabbed Julia by the wrist. Her voice determined, she said, "I'm not a bad woman, honey. I did what I had to do."

Julia's throat closed up. She no longer saw a mother who fought for her daughter, but a shriveled woman full of regret. Julia pulled her into a hug and whispered, "I know."

Once Jack and Julia got to her car, she got in, starting it up. She noticed that Jack was doing a quick reconnaissance of the area. "Anything?" she said.

"Doesn't appear to be," he said.

"Where to now?" she said.

"Let's go back to your place. I need to make some calls."

Julia drove without speaking, her mind recalling how defeated her mother seemed. Then she blurted, "Jack, do we really have to pursue this?"

"What do you mean?"

"With my mother. I don't think she's up to this and what will her statement really matter?"

"The more we know, the more ammunition we will have to prove that these guys were the men my dad said they were. And not just my dad, mind you. Remember Ron?"

"Who?"

"Ron, the bartender. Remember how the Kolson name set him off? It's the way many people feel about those bastards. They somehow manage to get away with, well, murder and no one can stop them."

Once they got back to the apartment, Jack said, "I'll be inside in a few, okay?"

"Okay," Julia said, watching as Jack strolled down the sidewalk, his cell phone to his ear. Before she unlocked her door, she heard him say, "Dad? How you doing?"

SIX

After they had some lunch, Jack and Julia went back to her mother's apartment. Julia rang the doorbell, but there wasn't an answer.

She then knocked, calling out, "Mom! It's us." When her mother didn't come to the door, Julia started to panic. Jack also started pounding on the door.

"I don't like this," she said, taking out her key. Her mother had given her a spare for emergencies. As far as Julia was concerned, this was an emergency.

She turned the chamber and unlocked the door, but when she opened it, the chain lock kept her from going any further.

"Mom!" Julia shouted. "Please, Mom." She didn't like what she was suspecting.

"I'm coming! I'm coming!" Ellen called, taking off the chain lock, opening the door.

Julia sighed with relief. "Why'd you have the chain on?" she said, as she and Jack came in.

Ellen locked the door behind them. "I just feel safer, that's all."

"You're afraid of what they might do, aren't you?" Jack said.

Ellen seemed to be stronger than she was earlier. She said, "It doesn't matter. I thought about it and I have to keep my word."

"Your word?" Jack said. "You mean to give us the statement?"

"No," Ellen said. "To keep my mouth shut. What's done is done and I cannot break my promise."

"Are you shittin' me!" Jack shouted.

"Jack!" Julia said. "Calm down."

"You'd better leave, Mr. Landry," Ellen said. "We don't use that language in this house."

"Maybe not," Jack said, "but you do hide the deeds of criminals."

Julia stood between her mother and Jack. "Let's just stop!" she shouted. "Mom, you told Jack you would give a statement."

"No, I did not. I said that I would think about it. And I did. And I say, no, I will not give a statement."

"Jesus," Jack said. He started pacing around the room.

"I think you had better leave," Ellen said. She went to her door and unlocked it.

Jack walked over and said, "You're never going to stop being afraid of those men, Mrs. Kolson, until we can get them in jail."

"It's not them I'm afraid of," she said. "It's you."

Jack darted out the door. Julia started to follow him, but then stopped, looking at her mother.

"And, Julia, I think you had better reconsider your relationship with that man. What do you really know about him?"

In reality, Julia didn't know a whole lot, but didn't say as much, and rushed to her car, sobbing uncontrollably.

Jack put out his hand. "Give me your keys. I'll drive."

She didn't argue with him and handed over the keys.

Instead of heading back to her apartment, Jack turned onto the parkway. "Let's go down to the beach," he said. "I don't feel like being cooped up."

Julia stared out the window. She'd stopped crying, but felt unmoored from everything she thought she knew.

What if her mother was right about Jack? After all, what did she, Julia, really know about him? Who was to say that the Kolsons were the ones in the wrong?

Maybe they did her mother and her a favor if they had killed Dennis. Her mother hadn't actually said as much, but she implied that he had abused her. What kind of life is that for anyone? The sudden touch of Jack's hand on hers caused her to jump.

"Sorry about before," he said. "I shouldn't have blown up like that."

"No, you shouldn't have. You certainly didn't gain any points with my mother."

After Jack found parking, they strolled down to the beach. It was crowded, filled with the sounds of children's laughter mixed with the crash of the ocean's waves. They took off their sandals, carrying them as they headed toward the water's edge.

"Let's walk," Jack said.

Julia strode alongside of him. "Jack, we can't ask my mother again. She's not going to help."

"You can't convince her?" he said.

"I'm not going to even try," she said.

Jack took her hand, and after a moment passed, he said, "I'd like you to come back to Philly with me."

"Why?"

"I'd like you to meet my father."

"I'm not ready to meet your father, Jack."

He let go of her hand. "I'm not bringing you home to my family as my girlfriend, Julia. I want you to meet my father. I think it's important."

"When?"

"How about we leave in the morning?"

Julia shrugged. "I guess so." There wasn't much keeping her on Long Island just now anyway.

"Good," he said. "And when we get back to your apartment, why don't you let me hang up those pictures for you?"

SEVEN

The next day when they reached Philadelphia, having taken Jack's vehicle, they went directly to his parents' house.

It was a small Dutch Colonial on a quiet, tree-lined street. He went up to the door and knocked. Moments later, an older woman answered.

"Jack, honey!" she said, pulling him into a hug.

"Hey, Mom, how you doing?"

She stepped back, holding him at arm's length. "Okay," she said, glancing at Julia.

"Oh, this is Julia," he said. "She's from Long Island."

"I wish you would've told me you were bringing company," she said, reaching up, touching the straggly gray strands of her hair and pushing them back.

"Sorry," he said.

"How do you do," Julia said, reaching over and gently shaking Mrs. Landry's hand. It felt fragile to her.

"Come in, dear," she said. "Would you like something to drink?"

"No, thank you. I'm fine."

"We came to see Dad," Jack said.

Mrs. Landry raised an eyebrow. "So, not your mother?"

Jack laughed. "That's not what I mean. I just wanted Julia to meet Dad. See, she's Dennis Kolson's daughter."

His mother's mouth dropped open. She turned a cool eye toward Julia. "Really?"

"She's not a Kolson, per se," he said.

"I never knew my father, Mrs. Landry."

"Probably just as well," Mrs. Landry said. She took a deep breath. "Let me go see if your father's awake." She left them standing in the foyer and went down the hallway.

"Welcome to my parents' humble abode," Jack said, forcing a grin.

Julia looked at her surroundings. The house was in need of repair, the hardwood floors dull and scratched. The furniture in the living room faded.

Mrs. Landry came back. "He's in the den. He's awake. A bit groggy, but awake."

"If we are disturbing him, Mrs. Landry, we can come back another time. Let him finish his nap."

"Oh, he's always napping these days," she said, leading them down the hall and into the den.

Julia followed Jack into the room to see Mr. Landry was in a hospital bed, his face pale and drawn, his eyes closed.

She looked at Jack, her expression stunned. It was unfair of him not to have warned her that his father was ill.

"Greg," Mrs. Landry said, her voice mellifluous, "you have company."

Mr. Landry opened his eyes. He searched the room until his sights landed on Jack. "My boy!" he said, his voice hoarse. "What brings you here today?"

"Hey, Dad," Jack said, walking over to the raised bed and giving his father a light hug. "Can't a guy visit his father for no reason?" He smiled.

"Sure." He caught sight of Julia. "Who's this pretty young girl?"

Jack turned toward Julia, bidding her to approach the bed. "Dad, this is Julia, she is Dennis Kolson's daughter."

Julia felt like a criminal just for being associated with a name that caused so much heartache. She wanted to say she was sorry, but her throat closed up.

Mr. Landry looked from her to Jack and then back to her, his forehead a corrugation of wrinkles. "Why'd you bring her here?" he said.

"I wanted her to hear our story."

Mr. Landry squeezed his eyes tight. "The Kolsons got away with murder and never paid for it," he said. He then stopped talking, his chest rising and falling ever so slightly.

"He's asleep," Mrs. Landry said. "He's so weak."

"Should we let him be for a while?" Jack said.

"I think so," Mrs. Landry said. "Come into the kitchen, I'll put on a pot of coffee."

"None for me, thanks," Julia said.

"Or me," Jack said.

They trailed behind Mrs. Landry into the kitchen. Jack went to the refrigerator and pulled out a bottle of cola. He looked over at Julia, asking if she'd want some.

She shook her head no. She didn't feel she had a right to anything from the Landry house. She said to Jack, "Has your dad been ill for long?"

"Yes, dear," Mrs. Landry interjected. "He's fought ulcers and migraines all his life. Now he's fighting pancreatic cancer." She leaned in. "Have you ever heard how anger can fester into disease?"

Julia didn't know how to reply, so said nothing.

"The man you just saw, he's been angry for most of his life, and much of it has to do with your family."

"They're not my family," Julia said, tears welling in her eyes. "I never knew them until just a few days ago."

Jack sat down with the soda bottle in his hand. He unscrewed it and began swilling down its contents, in spite of his mother's protests. "Get a glass, Jack!"

While he got up and went to the cabinet, Julia said, "Mrs. Landry, I don't really know why Jack brought me here, but I am sorry about all the pain you've had to deal with and the wrongdoing."

"Mom," Jack said, "you think Dad will have the strength to talk later?"

"I don't know, but what did you want to ask him?"

Jack mulled it over. "I guess there wasn't a whole lot more, really. I just wanted Julia to see that time is of essence. I want to give Dad his final wish, but will need her help."

"So, what have you two found out these last few days?" she said.

Jack proceeded to tell his mother about Julia finding the picture and how it snowballed into her going to Philly to look for her father's family, and the threatening phone call, followed by meeting with the Kolson men. And, of course, Julia's mother's revelations.

Mrs. Landry listened intently to the very end. She looked over at Julia. "I'm sorry I've been rude to you, but you have to understand the hell that family has put us through." She held up her finger to her lips as though to silence everyone, even though she was the only one speaking. "I thought I heard your father," she said. "I'll be right back." She got up and left Jack and Julia sitting at the kitchen table. When she returned, she said, "He was just mumbling. He does that quite a lot lately."

"So, your mother refuses to give a statement," she said.

Julia nodded.

"Perhaps it will help you to know that I was good friends with Katherine."

Julia gazed at her. "You were?"

Mrs. Landry nodded. "She's actually the one who introduced me to Jack's father."

"Oh," Julia said.

"Just a minute." Mrs. Landry got up, leaving the room. Julia assumed it was to check on Mr. Landry again, but she returned holding a stack of Polaroid photos. She started riffling through them, until she found one in particular. She handed it to Julia. It was of two young girls posing in front of the liberty bell.

"That's Katherine and me. We became inseparable." She went through some more photos and handed Julia another one. "Here's one of the surprise bridal shower she gave me."

"You were close."

"Yes, yes we were. And anything the Kolsons have to say about her being a gold digger is false."

Jack picked up the photos and started going through them while his mother continued talking.

"She did know your father, Julia. And, she did go out with him once or twice just to anger her father. It was nothing more than a lark to her, but Dennis was very good looking—young, but good looking. And he had money. She was flattered, and liked calling herself Mrs. Robinson."

"Mrs. Robinson?" Julia said.

"From the movie The Graduate."

Julia still didn't know what the reference meant.

"Anyway, Greg wasn't too happy about it, either, but he figured his sister was always so headstrong and if they just ignored it, she'd come to her senses. She'd get bored of him. After all, Dennis wasn't much more than a kid, a very misguided kid, mind you."

"What do you mean?" Julia said.

"He was obsessed with her. They hadn't really even what you would call dated, but he started calling her all of the time and getting angry with her when she ignored him. By then, I was busy raising Jack and trying to help Greg with his business so I didn't see her as much as I did when I was single. I mean, of course, we'd see each other at family gatherings and such, but she was still living the single life and I wasn't."

"Did she ever bring my Dad over?"

"Oh, goodness, no. She'd know better than that. Greg would have kicked him out. Besides, they weren't an item, so to speak."

"Mom?" Jack said, holding one of the photos. "Is this Aunt Katherine?"

Mrs. Landry took the photo. "Yes. That is her with her brand new truck. She loved that vehicle."

Jack handed it to Julia. "See anything?"

Julia looked closely. "Is this the Datsun you were talking about?"

Jack shook his head. He looked back at his mother. "We found a key for a Datsun in some of the things that Julia's father left behind."

Mrs. Landy frowned. "That's strange," she said.

"Maybe he had a Datsun, too," Julia said.

"Maybe," Jack said, studying the picture closely.

Just then, Mr. Landry called out to his wife. She got up to go to him and Jack followed. Julia wasn't sure what her place should be so she remained seated. She decided to look through the rest of the photos, finding pictures of Jack as a baby, which made her smile.

EIGHT

"Julia," Jack said, appearing around the corner. "He's awake. Why don't you come in?"

Julia tossed the photos back on to the table and went down to the den. Mrs. Landry was spoon feeding her husband ice chips.

"Here she is, Dad," Jack said, nudging Julia closer to the bed.

Mr. Landry reached out to her so she took his extended hand. It felt so cold.

"My son wants me to tell you some things," he whispered.

Julia nodded and said, "Okay."

"I don't bear any ill will 'gainst you," he said. "You gotta know that."

Julia looked over at Jack, who was standing next to her. He had his hand resting on his father's leg. "I know," she said.

"My sister had a whole life ahead of her," he said, a tear escaping from his eye. Mrs. Landry took a tissue and dabbed at it. "That night, the night she died," he said, "she was on her way to Mom and Dad's."

Mrs. Landry piped in, "Their parents, Jack's grandparents."

Julia nodded in understanding.

"I mean, we can't be sure, but that's the direction she was heading." He closed his eyes, his breathing labored.

"See," Mrs. Landry said, "the reason that matters is that she hadn't spoken to her parents for quite some time. They'd had a falling out."

"Because she was seeing a Kolson," Julia acknowledged.

Mr. Landry shook his head. "No, no. Her seeing that kid...just another thorn in the side."

"So, what was it, Dad?" Jack said, as if hearing the information for the first time.

"She had a full scholarship to college and threw it all away."

"She was very smart," Mrs. Landry said, "but she was also impatient."

"Wanted to get ahead without working for it. She would've been the first Landry to go to college. Mom and Dad were so disappointed in her when she gave it all up for a boy."

"My father?" Julia said.

"No," Mrs. Landry said. "Actually, he was a man and not a boy, like your father. But by the time they broke up, the scholarship was null and void."

Jack said, "How come I didn't know any of this? I was always told it was because she was seeing a Kolson that upset Grandma and Grandpa."

"Yes," Mrs. Landry said, "that did come to the forefront, after she died---"

"Murdered!" Mr. Landry spewed. "She was murdered." He started coughing uncontrollably.

Once he settled back down, Mrs. Landry continued talking. "I suppose it helped to blame it on something else when you are in so much pain. They regret that they never reconciled with their daughter. Not going to college seemed like nothing after she was murdered."

"Mom," Jack said, "what made us think that she was pregnant?"

Mrs. Landry's expression changed. She glanced at her husband, whose face got rigid. She said, "Your aunt came over one day, just when she was starting to hang out with Dennis. She'd been dating someone else, but had just broken up with him. She told me that she...she was late, you know, with her monthly. Then she said that she'd even told Dennis." Mrs. Landry looked away, but then sputtered, "Even though they never had...relations...he started telling people he'd gotten her pregnant, that he was going to be a father."

"And the Kolsons believed him," Jack said.

Mrs. Landry nodded and motioned toward Mr. Landry. "He paid the family a visit, tried to tell them otherwise, but things just got out of hand after all that."

"I'd say they did," Jack said, his voice getting louder. "Why didn't you tell me all this? You knew I have been nosing around, probing for answers."

"Because someone killed my sister. That I know for sure. Mom and Dad never got to make things right with her and went to their graves with that burden. I don't want to go the same way."

"Mr. Landry," Julia said, "how do you know that the Kolsons were responsible for her going off that bridge?"

"Because your father told me. And then they offed him to keep him quiet. Killed their own brother to shut him up."

Julia was having a difficult time making sense of everything. It seemed there were lies and fabrications all around. She noticed then that Mr. Landry had drifted off into a sound sleep.

"Come on," Jack said, taking her hand and leading her out of the room. "This is getting too much for him." To his mother, he said, "We're going to go and let Dad rest."

"Don't you want to stay for supper?" she said.

"No. I have so much I need to sort out."

"Jack, please, don't be angry with me," she said, following them down the hallway to the front door. "I didn't mean to keep so much from you, and your aunt didn't do anything wrong except get mixed up with the wrong family."

"It was more than that, Mom," he said.

Mrs. Landry bit her lip.

"It was nice meeting you," Julia said.

Mrs. Landry gave her a slight smile. "This isn't how we usually entertain," she said.

Jack and Julia walked out, heading toward the vehicle when Jack shouted, "Shit!"

"What?" she said.

He ran over to the vehicle, looking at the front and rear tires on the driver's side. Both were flat.

"Oh my gosh," Julia said.

Jack looked up and down the street. "This was a message," he said.

"Maybe we ran over some glass."

"Glass?" he said, sneering. "Wake up, Julia. We are getting close to some answers and someone doesn't like it."

"I cannot take this," she said, wishing she'd never had taken the box of her father's things from her mother's house. "I just want to go home and forget about everything."

NINE

Later that evening, after Jack fixed the tires, they headed back to Long Island. The whole ride, Jack kept looking in the rearview mirror, keeping Julia on edge.

It wasn't until they were on the Jersey Turnpike that Julia spoke. "Can we just go over the facts? I mean, I am so confused, I don't know what is what."

Jack pounded the steering wheel. "Same here! It seems people on all sides have secrets."

"Okay," Julia said, "what we know for sure is Dennis didn't get your aunt pregnant and quite likely she wasn't, if we are to believe the autopsy report."

"And maybe she was heading to my grandparents to let them know she wasn't pregnant when she went off the bridge," Jack added.

"Why would a seventeen year-old kid be willing to say he got your aunt pregnant?"

"Cocky, probably. She was a very attractive woman, Julia. I'm sure he thought it would make him look more like a man and he boasted about it to everyone."

"So, it sounds like she never tried to pin it on him and Dale and Donald were wrong about her being a gold digger."

"I guess so," Jack said.

"But why would they kill her? I mean, wouldn't she tell them the truth?"

"Unless they didn't give her a chance."

Julia stared out the window at the sky filling with lights from the passing buildings. Then something suddenly occurred to her. She said, "You know, I don't recall my mother ever telling me just how she did meet my father."

Jack glanced in her direction. "Really?"

"No. I mean, what brought him to Long Island? Or was she in Philadelphia?"

"Think it's too late to go over there to ask her?"

Julia looked at the time. It was nearing nine o'clock. "I'll give her a call and tell her we want to stop by."

"Make sure she knows it's not to ask for a statement."

Julia brought her mother's number up on her cell phone. It rang four times until it went to her answering machine. "Mom, it's Julia. Please answer. Jack and I would like to stop in. We're not going to ask you for a statement, I promise." She waited, hoping her mother was screening her call and would eventually pick up. "Mom, please answer." Then, she concluded, "We'll be there in about forty minutes. Love you."

"Where do you think she is?"

Julia shrugged. "It's rare that she goes out at night. Maybe playing bingo with some friends. Sometimes she does that."

She'd tried to call a second time when they were around the block, but it went to the answering machine once again. The apartment was on the first floor and there didn't appear to be any lights on.

Julia looked in her mother's designated parking spot. "That's her car," she said to Jack.

"Maybe someone picked her up," he said.

She knocked on the door and waited, and then knocked again.

"If she's in there, she's really pissed off at us," Jack said.

Julia took out her key, hoping the chain lock wasn't on. To her relief, it wasn't. They walked in with Julia feeling on the wall for the light switch. She turned it on. Nothing seemed to be amiss.

"Mom?" she called, walking down the hall toward the bedroom. The door was closed.

She opened it and found the switch on the wall, turning on the light. There was her mother in bed, her eyes opened but empty, her body lifeless.

"Mom!" Julia shrieked, running over to her. She lifted her mother's body and hugged it, repeatedly calling out her name.

EPISODE 3

ONE

Jack had dialed 911, even though it was clear it was much too late for an ambulance.

By the time the police and EMT arrived, Julia was sitting in the living room, feeling shell shocked. Jack was telling the police how they'd found Mrs. Kolson in bed. He lowered his voice, but Julia could still hear him tell the cop that foul play may have been involved.

Her eyes wide, she got up to where they were standing, and said, "So you think they were here?"

The police officer asked who.

"The Kolsons," she replied.

Jack gave a brief overview about the powerful family from Philadelphia and how they were connected to Ellen Kolson. He concluded, "Doubtful it was them personally, but they could've sent someone."

"But she was being so careful," Julia said. "She kept the door chain locked and--"

Jack interrupted her. "The chain lock wasn't on," he said. "Otherwise, we wouldn't have been able to get inside."

Julia gasped. "That wouldn't have been like her." She looked around the room to find any other evidence, but all that she suddenly noticed was the box of doughnuts that she'd brought for their breakfast together were still on the table. They had to have been stale by now, she thought. Still, she didn't throw them out.

Several hours later, after the body had been removed, the house dusted for fingerprints and an autopsy ordered, Julia and Jack sat bleary eyed at the dining room table absorbing all that had just transpired.

"According to the detective, none of the neighbors said they saw anyone suspicious around here," Jack said.

"It's my fault," Julia said. "I started this whole thing and now my mother is---" She couldn't say the word so she left it unspoken.

"Don't go blaming yourself," Jack said. He glanced at the clock on the wall. "It's after four o'clock. We need to get some sleep."

"I don't know if I can."

"We've got a busy day ahead of us," he said. "Arrangements have to be made and I'm sure you'll have people to call."

Julia rested her head on the table. "I want it all to stop."

Jack stood up. "Come on, let's get you home. You need to sleep. We should have some answers in a few hours."

***

Julia woke up around ten a.m. She lay in bed trying to remember what had happened the night before when it hit her: Her mother was gone. The very idea didn't make sense.

She turned to see that the other side of the bed was empty and hurriedly tossed off the covers.

She ran down the hallway wearing only her undergarments looking for Jack. She found him in the kitchen on his cell phone. He was sitting at the table with a cup of coffee in front of him.

"Okay," he said, "I'll let her know. Thanks." He hung up and looked at Julia. "According to the pathologist, it was an aortic aneurysm."

"So...," she said.

"So that means there's no proof that the Kolsons were somehow involved with this."

"At least not directly."

"Doesn't appear to be, but we'll wait for the lab to get back to us on the fingerprints they lifted." He pointed to the coffee pot on the counter. "It's still hot," he said.

She nodded. "Let me get something on first."

When she returned wearing a pair of jeans and navy blue blouse there was a cup of coffee and a plate of buttered toast waiting on the table for her. She sat down and took a sip. "So it had to be the shock of everything that killed her."

"You don't know that," Jack said,

"But, Jack, don't forget," Julia said, "the chain lock was off."

"I mentioned that again to the detective," he said.

"And?"

Jack sighed. "He said that often when people have an intuition something isn't quite right they make it easier for the family in any way they can. He thinks your mother may have purposely left the chain lock off so that you could get to her without too big of a problem."

"Oh, I don't know," she said, biting into a slice of toast, chewing and swallowing.

Jack said, "Also, the body is ready for release."

TWO

After finishing her breakfast, somehow Julia managed to make arrangements with a funeral home.

She had never had to do any such thing before and it felt surreal while talking about her mother in the past tense to the director. After all, it would have been her mother who would have helped with the uncomfortable, new experience had she not been dead.

Hanging up, Julia said to Jack, "I have to go back to the apartment to get an outfit for her."

"Good," he said, "I need to go back there anyway."

"Why?"

"To check the phone and answering machine, see what calls came in or what calls went out."

"Oh," she said. "I never thought of that. I'll call Aunt Barb from here. She's my mom's sister."

Julia's aunt was heartbroken by the news. "I always thought I'd see Ellen again," she said. "She's just too young for this." She sniffled, and then added, "I'll be there as soon as I can."

Julia didn't know her aunt that well. Living across the country from each other wasn't conducive for a close relationship.

Whenever Julia suggested to her mother that they should take the trip, Ellen said that she couldn't afford it. Now, that seemed like another lie she'd left Julia to consider.

She and Jack headed over to the apartment. At first Julia started to knock on the door, but then remembered no one would answer.

She used her key and let herself and Jack inside. Jack went immediately to the phone. Julia followed in anticipation.

The answering machine had 0 unheard calls, so he then hit star 69, handing his notepad and pen to Julia. The last number had a local area code.

He repeated it aloud to Julia who jotted it down, but instead of dialing it, he hit redial. The number that came up had a 215 area code.

"Bingo," he said.

"What do you mean?" Julia drew closer to him, hearing the phone ring. She heard the click and then some man's voice, but couldn't make out what he said.

Jack responded, "No, this isn't Ellen. Uh, who is this? Yes, I know I called you, but I have sad news to share and want to know who I'm telling." He paused, listening, and then replied, "I'm calling on behalf of Ellen's daughter. Yes, yes, Julia." There was another pause with Jack starting to pace and listening intently. "I really can't share the information I have until I know who this is."

Julia heard an angry, "Go to hell!" before there was the disconnected click.

Jack looked to be thinking. He said, "What's that local number you wrote down?" Julia handed him the paper and he punched the number into his cell phone. Moments later, he disconnected without having spoken to anyone. He said, "Nails Are Us."

"Oh," Julia said, "yes, my mom goes there every week for a manicure." Then she hesitated and corrected herself. "Went there."

"Someone in Philly recognized your mother's number."

"What do you mean?"

"Instead of greeting me with a hello, he said your mother's name. I'm going to have to investigate this number. I'll need to head back to your place and use your computer."

"Just let me pick out some clothes for my mom first," she said, heading down to her mother's bedroom.

She stopped outside in the hallway, not wanting to look at the bed, and began sobbing. How could she possibly do what she was about to do? The weight of finding an outfit for someone to wear for all eternity seemed bizarre to Julia.

Suddenly she jumped at someone touching her shoulder. She screamed only to discover it was Jack.

"It's just me, babe," he said, pulling her into a hug. "It's just me."

Julia let him hold her for several minutes until she could collect herself. Only then did she go to her mother's closet and pushed one dress after the next to the side, from right to left, finding nothing she thought worked.

It was the first time she realized just how frugal her mother had actually lived. She couldn't have gotten that great of a payoff from the Kolsons, Julia thought.

Eventually, she settled on a navy blue polyester dress and some simple black pumps. For some reason, she remembered the director telling her to bring shoes, as well as undergarments. It was all so strange to Julia.

"Okay," she said to Jack, "I think this is it. We can drop this off and then head back to my place."

Once Jack and Julia returned to her apartment, Jack went directly to the computer while Julia went to her bedroom and fell onto her bed.

She realized she had so much work to do since she needed to find an insurance policy, bank records, and, perhaps, a will.

She had no idea where to begin and found it was easier just to curl up in a ball and pretend she was in a nightmare and would eventually wake up where all was well with the world.

"Well, I figured as much," Jack said, coming into the bedroom and laying down next to her.

She rolled over, facing him. "What?"

"The phone number was unlisted, but the area code is from the vicinity of Philly that I expected."

"But she called them," Julia said. "Why do you suppose?"

"Could be any number of reasons, but we might be able to find some things out if we can find her paperwork." He draped an arm across Julia. "Did your mom ever tell you where she kept all her important documents?"

"No. And I never asked. It's just...well...I never expected I would need any of that for a long, long time."

"I don't want to push you, babe, but I think we need to go back there and see what we can find."

"I'm just so tired," Julia said.

"I know."

Sucking up some air, she sat up. "Okay, let's do this. If anything, hopefully I'll find a policy that will pay for the funeral expenses. I can't believe how much this'll cost me."

THREE

When they first got back to her mother's apartment, Julia had little idea where to begin. At first Jack stood behind her while she was rifling through the desk drawers in the spare bedroom until she gave him permission to go on his own search.

"I'm not sure I feel comfortable doing that, Julia. This is very personal."

"Please," she said, "I could use help. I'm just trying to think where my mom would hide those kinds of documents."

Just then she found a checkbook. She opened it to see how much was in it. "Four thousand two dollars," she said. "That's not a lot."

"Certainly not for someone being paid to keep quiet," Jack said. "There has to be something more somewhere."

"Yeah, check the closets," Julia said. She continued going through the desk, scooping out receipts for paid bills, birthday cards from over the years and a collection of pens and pencils.

She started to toss everything on the floor until the drawers were empty. Once everything was in a pile, she sat down and went through it gradually, one item after the next.

She never considered her mother to be a packrat of any sort, but she did seem to hang on to receipts for bills for quite a number of years.

Jack walked in. "Nothing, as far as I can tell," he said, sitting down across from her. He started going through the piles with her.

"This is crazy," Julia started to say when she came to a sealed letter-size envelope with her name scrolled across it. She looked up at Jack while ripping it open. Inside were a small key and a signature card with Julia's handwriting.

"I don't recall ever signing this," she said.

"What's the note say?"

Julia looked down at the piece of paper that had fallen on to her lap. She read, "For safe deposit box number 312 at Roslyn Savings. Oh my gosh," she said, "this may be it."

"Let's go," Jack said, looking at his watch. "They'll be closing soon." He stood up. "Do you know which bank that is?" He helped Julia up off the floor.

Grasping the envelope, she said, "It's the only bank my Mom ever used." Then she stopped for a moment as if recalling something. "You know, she'd opened an account for me there when I was just a kid. I think it was for my tenth birthday, but I forgot all about that. I wonder what happened with that."

"Let's see what we can find out," Jack said, taking her by the hand. They started to head out the door when the phone rang.

Scowling, Jack went over and looked at the screen. He shouted to Julia, "Answer this and pretend you are your mother!"

"What?" Julia said. "I can't--"

"It's that guy! From Philly! It's the only way we'll find out."

Julia tried to calm herself down before picking up the receiver. She affected the best Ellen Kolson voice that she could while watching Jack run down the hall to the bedroom where there was an extension. "Hello," she said.

"Ellen," the male voice said. "I just want to let you know that someone was nosing around. I think it was that reporter you told me about."

Playing along, Julia said, "Really, what makes you think that?"

"Your daughter must've let him in your house when you weren't home."

"I...I told him I wasn't going to give any statement, you have to believe that."

"My son's political career could be ruined because of this. We've managed to keep this, this situation out of the public for years and it has to stay that way. Next year is a big year for the Kolsons and we cannot have anything jeopardize that. "

Trying to respond how her mother would have, she said, "I will tell my daughter that he's no good, that she cannot see him."

"You could have discouraged her from trying to meet her father's family."

Julia's hand was shaking. "I tried, but she was so insistent. I didn't think she'd get very far."

"Well, apparently Landry has been helping her. And she, him. But let me remind you, your daughter has Kolson blood in her."

"What do you mean?" Julia said, her voice suddenly betraying her.

There was silence on the other end of the line.

"Hello," she said, gathering herself.

"Just remember this," he said, "Dennis didn't have to die." He then hung up.

Julia placed the phone back down, her entire being trembling. She said to Jack as he came down the hall, "Who do you think that was?"

"I believe you just had a conversation with David Kolson."

"He doesn't know that my mother died," she said. "Which means they probably didn't do it."

Jack looked to be considering it, and then said, "Listen, let's just get to the bank and see if we can find anything out that way. We'll figure this out later."

Julia directed him on how to get to Roslyn Savings, which was less than a mile away, while Jack reminded her that she had every right to have access to the box and to act accordingly. And, by all means, don't mention that your mother died."

"Why?" she said.

"Just see what's in that box first," he said.

He pulled up to the entrance to drop her off.

"Aren't you coming in with me?" she said.

"I won't be allowed, but take what you think is important for now."

Still shaking from the phone call and feeling like she was breaking some law, Julia climbed out of the car and went into the bank. Fortunately, there was an officious looking woman there to greet her.

"I'd like to get to my safety deposit box," Julia said, holding the key and signature card.

"Sure, right this way."

Julia followed the banker who unlocked the door to the room. She realized she would look suspicious when she had no idea which direction she was to go, but the banker took her card, looked at it and led her directly to number 312.

"Here you are," she said, unlocking the safe.

Julia's heart sank, at first believing that the banker was not going to leave. Instead, the woman pulled out the box, and handed it to Julia. She then started to walk away, but when Julia stayed in place, the woman turned and said, "Don't you want to go in here?" She pointed to a door.

"Oh, yes," Julia said, following the banker who gave her entrance to a small empty room with a table and chair.

"Just let us know when you are done," the banker said, leaving Julia in the room.

"Okay," she said, waiting for the door to close. She placed the box on the table and took her key, hoping it fit. It did.

She lifted off the cover and discovered envelopes all marked with information. As she went through the items, she was relieved to find that there was an insurance policy and a will.

She was hoping there would also be a letter revealing the secret her mother held but that didn't appear to be the case.

The words "your daughter has Kolson blood in her" haunted her. What did that strange caller mean by that?

She fit the documents and some other paperwork she'd go through when she got back home into her purse, leaving the box empty.

She carried it back to the vault and slipped it into the empty slot, closing it, which automatically locked. When she walked out of the vault, the banker said cheerfully, "That it for today?"

"Yes, yes, thank you," Julia said, going out to the parking lot. Immediately, Jack pulled up and she climbed in.

"How'd it go?" he said.

"Looks like she did have a will and a policy."

"Let's head back to your place, order take out and start going through everything, okay?"

"Okay," she said. "I am starving."

FOUR

While Jack and Julia were eating a mushroom pizza, intermittently wiping sauce from their hands, they went through the items that Julia had taken from the safe deposit box.

They found that everything would go to her, thanks to the will her mother had left; it was just a matter of Julia contacting the lawyer.

The insurance policy was updated and Julia was stunned to learn that she would have far more than enough money to pay for the funeral expenses.

"Anything else?" Jack said, picking through the papers that she'd taken from her purse. They found her parents' marriage certificate and a booklet with Julia's name on it.

"Oh, this is from when my mom opened up the bank account for me in my name." She opened the book and scowled.

"What? What is it?"

Julia handed it over to him with a gentle laugh. "Thank goodness for the insurance policy," she said.

Jack opened the booklet. "Twelve dollars and nine cents."

She took a final bite of her pizza, picked up the plate and brought it to the dishwasher. "You know, I don't even know who's going to show up tomorrow. When the funeral director asked me if I wanted to list Mom's obituary in the paper, I said sure. But he said he'd need some information from me before he could do that and I never got it to him."

"Hmm," Jack said, "I don't mean to sound cold, but that may be just as well. I think the longer we can wait for the Kolsons to find out that your mother died the better."

"Not many people are going to be showing up for the wake," she said, starting to cry. That's when she realized that she should tell Kevin. After all, he'd been Ellen's son-in-law for several years. Quite likely, he'd want to know.

Julia wiped away the tears, found her cell phone and while his number was ringing, she dropped down on to the couch feeling wiped out.

When her ex picked up, she didn't start with small talk, but blurted, "Kevin, Mom died." And she began to sob all over again.

There was a long pause before Kevin snapped, "Julia, I'm sorry, but I am getting married on Saturday. Why would you call me with this now?"

Taken aback, she replied, "I'd just thought you'd want to know. She did consider you to be a family member."

"Well, we're no longer a family. I'm sorry for your loss, but please don't try to ruin any more of my happiness. Bye."

Julia threw the phone across the room. How dare he? She attempted to process what had just transpired.

Jack was sitting at the desk working on the computer. "I'm guessing that didn't go too well."

"No," she said, her tears having stopped. "He really is an asshole."

Jack got up and went over to sit with her on the couch. "It's late, why don't we call it a night so we're prepared for the wake?" He then sighed in exasperation. "Ah, shit, I don't have anything to wear. I only packed jeans and casual shirts."

"I don't think it's going to matter, Jack. Besides my aunt, I don't know who else will be there."

"Well, I'd like to make a good impression on your aunt then," he said, taking Julia's hand. "When does she get in, by the way?"

"She said she'd get here as soon as she could. I gave her my address and the funeral home's address."

"Is anyone coming with her?"

"She didn't say. I never met her husband or kids."

Jack scowled. "Why not?"

Julia shrugged. "I always assumed it was because she lived across the country. Mom never said anything bad about her. Actually, she never said much at all about her."

"How well do you know her?"

"She and her husband came to my wedding. That was the first time we met."

"How was she and your mom? Did they seem to get along?"

Another shrug. "I guess. I was so caught up in getting married that I didn't pay attention to how they interacted. She did sound really sad on the phone, though, when I told her Mom had died."

Jack stood, went over to pick Julia's phone off the floor. "Well, I'll head over to the mall in the morning to pick something up. There's only one viewing, right?" He handed her the phone.

"Yes, tomorrow night at seven and the funeral is the next day."

"Then that gives me plenty of time," he said.

"And while you're doing that I think I'll go over to my mother's and look up names from her address book to let her friends know."

Jack nodded. "If Kolson calls while you're there see if you can get more information from him. I'd like to know what he meant about next year being a big year for the Kolsons."

FIVE

Early the next evening, Julia and her Aunt Barb walked together into the funeral home with Jack trailing a bit behind. "You go on ahead," he'd said, not wanting to intrude on their grief.

Julia had managed to call a couple of her mother's friends whose names and numbers she'd found in the address book. Shocked and saddened, they each promised to pass along the message.

"It's short notice," said Mary, her mother's bingo partner, "but I'll do my best."

Julia had thanked her and hoped that there would at least be a small gathering mourning the woman who was going to her grave with deep secrets.

Julia and her aunt stood by the casket, holding each other's hand. They only let go to wipe away their tears.

Julia thought her mother looked angry with the way her mouth was turned down. Aunt Barb kept repeating, "Dear, dear Ellen. Why so soon? Why?"

When they went to take a seat, Jack sat down next to Julia. Over the two-hour time slot, several of her mother's friends did show up, offer their condolences, said what a wonderful cook Ellen was, how she was so generous with her time, and so on.

"She loved you," Mary said to Julia. "She was always telling us how proud she was of you."

Julia felt her heart sink, wishing she'd been on better terms with her mother before she'd died.

The next day the funeral service, if one could call it that, took place at the funeral home since she and her mother hadn't belonged to any church.

It was just Jack, Julia, Aunt Barb and Mary in attendance.

The funeral director read some quotes from the Bible, asked if anyone wanted to say anything in Ellen's honor, which no one did, and then led the way to the cemetery.

After they all tossed sand on the coffin and said their goodbyes, Julia found it difficult to leave.

How could this be it?

Aunt Barb and Jack had to gently guide her to the car.

They went back to her mother's house where Mary had arranged to have some cold cuts and salads delivered.

Later that afternoon, it was just Julia, her aunt and Jack sitting in the living room. Julia felt like an orphan and yearned to belong to someone.

She said, "Aunt Barb, I wish you lived closer."

Aunt Barb gave Julia a sad smile. "That would've been nice. I think you would have gotten along with your cousins."

"Mom never talked about you much."

Aunt Barb looked down, straightening the hem of her dress. "She was angry with me, Julia, for a very long time."

"Why?"

Aunt Barb sighed and looked over at Jack, who stood and said he needed to go for a walk. "I'll let you two catch up." Just then, his cell phone rang and he said, "Good timing" before walking out the front door.

"So what happened between the two of you?" Julia said.

"Oh, I don't even know if I should hash it all out now. It's water under the bridge."

"Did you go to Mom's wedding?"

Aunt Barb, cocked an eyebrow, and replied with aloofness, "What wedding?"

Julia went to the edge of the couch. "Mom's and my dad's." She pointed over to the photo on the shelf.

"Oh, they had that picture taken after the fact. They got married by a Justice of the Peace."

"Did Grandma and Grandpa go?" Julia said, realizing how little she knew about her mother's young life.

Aunt Barb snorted. "I should say not. They didn't think it was a good idea."

"Why?"

"Well, because of your father."

"Was he abusive to her before they were married?" Julia said.

"Oh, I don't know about any abuse," Aunt Barb said, getting up and heading to the kitchen with her empty wine glass. "They just felt that he wasn't…"

Julia didn't hear the last of her aunt's sentence and jumped up off the couch and headed into the kitchen. "He wasn't what?"

"He shouldn't have been released, that's how we all felt. Granted, I was a couple years younger than your mother, but I could tell that something wasn't quite right with him."

"He was in jail?" Julia said wide-eyed.

"Jail?" Aunt Barb shook her head. "Not that I know of. No, he'd been in Pilgrim State Hospital. That's how your mother met him."

"Pilgrim State Hospital?" Julia said. "That's for…for…"

"The criminally insane, psychotics, mentally ill," Aunt Barb said, pouring herself another glass of wine. "Your mother had been volunteering there. She'd wanted to be some sort of counselor and thought the experience would be helpful."

"She never told me that." Julia followed her aunt back to the living room. They both sat down where they'd sat before.

"Well, it didn't pan out the way she'd intended. The hospital apparently told her she was not to fraternize with the patients, but she didn't listen. She said she was in love and that Dennis shouldn't have been put in there in the first place. Somehow he managed to get released and ended up with your mother."

"So, he was crazy," Julia said.

"Your Mom didn't tell my Mom and Dad how she'd met him, but when the hospital called them, warning them with their concerns, Ellen was furious. She packed her things, moved out, apparently went to the Justice of the Peace and married your father right away."

"What did you do?"

"I was heading off to Stanford University. I thought she was being pretty impetuous, but just in love. At the time, I thought it was romantic what she was doing for love. What did I know?"

"So, did you go to my father's funeral?"

"No, but Mom and Dad did. That is when they reconciled with Ellen."

"So why was she angry with you?"

"Because I moved away and wasn't around to help when she had you. Of course, Mom was excited when she found out she was going to be a grandmother."

"I don't really have a lot of memories of Grandma and Grandpa," Julia said.

"You poor girl," Aunt Barb said. "You really were cut off from everybody, weren't you?"

Julia's eyes filled with tears. She got up to excuse herself for a minute and went down the hall to the bathroom.

Everything was just too much to take. She suddenly realized just how angry she was with her mother for keeping so much from her. She took a tissue and blew her nose.

Just as she was ready to walk out of the bathroom, the phone rang. On the second ring she heard her aunt say, "Hello."

"Who is this? Ellen? Oh, I'm her sister and I'm sorry to be the one to have to tell you this--"

Suddenly, it dawned on Julia just who the caller could be. She ran toward her aunt, shouting, "No, no! Don't say anything!"

Scowling, her aunt turned her back to Julia. "She passed away. The funeral was today. Hello? Hello?" She put the phone down, turning to Julia. "What a strange call."

"Who was it?" Julia said, hoping it was anyone other than the one she suspected.

"He refused to say," Aunt Barb said. "I wonder if he was someone your mother was seeing."

Julia looked at the caller I.D., recognizing the 215 area code. The front door opened. It was Jack returning. Julia fixed her eyes on him. She said, "He called again." Jack looked over at where Aunt Barb was standing. Julia added, "Now he knows Mom is dead."

"What is going on?" Aunt Barb said.

That's when Julia and Jack filled her in about Julia's search for her father and all that followed.

Aunt Barb's expressions went from curiosity to shock to horror throughout their conversation. Once they concluded, she had finished her second glass of wine and went back for a refill. Upon her return, she said, "I'm so sorry if I put you in danger. Those Kolsons sound downright frightening."

"I guess that's why Mom was so scared all these years."

"It also explains why she never had to hold down a job," Aunt Barb said.

"I just don't know what secret she was forced to keep," Julia said.

"You know," Aunt Barb said, "something struck me about your conversation that was odd. You'd said that your father left home after that older woman was killed, right?"

Julia nodded.

"But I wonder how he ended up at Pilgrim State on Long Island then."

Jack perked up. "What do you mean?"

"Oh," Julia said, "while you were outside, Aunt Barb told me that is how Mom met Dennis. He was a patient at Pilgrim State here on Long Island."

Aunt Barb looked over at Jack and did the universal crazy sign with her hand.

"I doubt that he'd admit himself," Jack said. "Someone put him in there, but the question is, why?"

At that moment, Julia gasped. "Oh my gosh, do you think that's what David Kolson meant when he said I have the Kolson blood in me?"

"Could be," Jack said.

Julia swallowed hard. For the last few weeks she'd hoped to find out if there was a genetic medical reason why she wasn't able to conceive. She never thought that mental illness could be a possibility.

"Julia," Jack said, "I know what you're thinking and you are not crazy."

"But I threw my phone across the room the other day. Remember? I overreacted!"

Jack and Aunt Barb burst into laughter, which caused Julia to break down and cry. She exclaimed, "It's not funny!"

Jack went over to her, putting an arm around her. "Honey, any possible symptoms would've shown themselves by now." He kissed her on the forehead. "But I think we might be onto something."

"What do you mean?" Julia said.

"If there is mental illness in a family, it doesn't make for a secure political career." He looked to be thinking. "I have some research to do. Mind if I go back to your place and jump on the computer?"

Julia looked over at her aunt. "Did you want to stay with us? I have a spare room."

"Oh, sweetie, that would be lovely, but I booked a room at The Holiday Inn and have an early flight out in the morning. However, if it's not too much trouble, could you drop me off on your way home?"

SIX

It had been a long day. While Jack went on Julia's computer, she went directly to bed.

She was sorry she didn't have more time to spend with her aunt, but they'd promised to stay in touch. "You visit me soon, okay?" her aunt had said, giving her a tight hug when she was dropped off at the hotel.

Julia fell asleep with the memory of feeling a little less orphaned.

The next morning she woke up feeling refreshed. She looked over to see that Jack hadn't been to bed all night.

She got up, slipping on a bathrobe, and went down the hall to the living room. He wasn't there. Nor was he in the kitchen.

Then she spotted that a note pad was pressed up against the computer with a scribbled message: On the trail. Heading back to Philly. Call me as soon as you read this. Love, Jack

Julia found her cell phone and immediately called Jack. To her dismay, it went directly to his voicemail so she left a message.

She looked at the note again. Love, Jack. It made her smile.

She went into the kitchen to make herself some breakfast. While she was eating her Cheerios and sipping on orange juice, she started to make a list of all the things she needed to do.

She'd have to call the lawyer and the insurance company that had her mother's policy.

Grateful that she was on summer break and had the time, she would also have to clean out her mother's apartment.

Who knows what else I might find, she thought. Once she finished the list and her breakfast, she went to take a shower, wondering why Jack hadn't returned her call.

By mid-afternoon when Jack still hadn't gotten back to her, she began to panic. The idea that he was on the trail could mean that the Kolsons were well aware of it, especially since they now knew that it hadn't been her mother David Kolson had spoken to on the phone. She decided to try him for a fourth time.

"Hello?" said a tentative male voice. Julia knew it wasn't Jack's.

"Who is this?" she said.

"Who is this?" the male parroted.

"Where's Jack?" she demanded.

Click.

"Jack!" she shouted. "Jack?"

Without giving it another thought, she threw some clothes in an overnight bag and set off for Philly, having little idea just where she'd be going.

However, she figured that he was now at the Kolsons' mercy and she refused to let them take away her future with this man.

By the time she got to the city proper, she decided she didn't have any other choice but to go to the Dale Kolson headquarters. It was risky, but she needed to find Jack.

Parking wasn't easy, but eventually she found a lot a couple blocks away. Feeling shaky but determined, she pushed through the door.

Gail Ryan, the receptionist, looked up from her desk. She was on the phone and pointed to an empty chair for Julia to take. Instead, Julia impatiently approached the desk.

"Yes," Gail said. "Um, but could we continue this conversation later? I have a visitor. An out-of-town visitor." Julia watched Gail closely, listening to what she was saying. "Yes," Gail said," that's right." She then hung up.

"Good afternoon, Ms...Ms.--"

"It's Julia. Where's Jack Landry?"

Gail sighed and stood up. "I don't know what you are talking about, Julia." She walked over to a water cooler and filled up a paper cup. "Would you care for some?" she said, patting the cooler.

Julia shook her head. "No. I have reason to believe that the Kolsons did something with him. If I don't start getting answers, I'm going to go to the police."

"Why would you think that they have anything to do with that third-rate reporter?" Gail said.

"I think you know why," Julia replied, hearing the door behind her open. She turned to see a man standing there. She thought he looked somewhat familiar, but wasn't sure why.

"Buy any more Guinness for your boyfriend?" he said.

She stared at him, remembering him from the parking lot when she'd gone grocery shopping back on Long Island.

"Why don't you come with me?" he said.

Julia backed away. "I'd rather not."

"You don't have a choice," he said, patting the blazer of his pocket.

It didn't escape Julia what he was implying. She said, "So your goons are going to have me killed, too, just to keep me quiet? You know, too many people already know what's going on." She looked over her shoulder at Gail, who seemed to be calmly observing.

Feeling trapped, she knew she had no escape and allowed the man to bring her outside to where an SUV was waiting.

"Get in and I wouldn't try to run, if I were you."

She climbed up onto the seat and he shut the door behind her. He watched her closely as he got into the driver's side. He immediately locked all the doors and pulled onto the street.

"Will I see Jack?" she said.

The man shrugged. "You'll get some answers upon our destination." He turned on the car radio. Bruce Springsteen blasted from the speakers.

SEVEN

Julia tried to pay attention to where he was bringing her, not at all familiar with the City of Brotherly Love.

They sat in traffic since it seemed everyone was leaving work. She wanted to bang on the windows and scream for help, but the music was too loud and windows tinted where no one could see inside.

About thirty minutes later, they were in a more suburban area. The SUV pulled into a circular driveway and approached a large brick colonial home.

He stopped at the front steps, turned off the engine. Finally, silence. He got out and came around, opening the door for Julia.

"Come on," he said, leading her up the steps to the front door. He rang the doorbell and not much later they were greeted by a young woman who was dressed in scrubs.

"Hey, John" she said. "Mr. Kolson is expecting you." She looked at Julia. "Hi," she said. "I'm Karen, Mr. Kolson's nurse."

Julia no longer felt threatened. She said hello and followed Karen and the man, whose name she just learned was John, down the lengthy hallway.

The home was spacious, the hardwood floors gleaming. They passed by walls covered with family photos, but she wasn't given time to scrutinize any of them.

Karen pushed open some French doors and led them into a room that smelled of Lysol.

Sitting near some floor-to-ceiling windows looking out over a garden was an old man hunkered down in a wheelchair. Slowly, he turned to face them. He motioned for Karen and John to leave.

Once they closed the doors behind them, the old man said, "So, you are the granddaughter I'd never met."

Even though he appeared feeble, he sounded strong and confident. Julia took a step closer. So this was David Kolson. She said, "Where's Jack?"

David Kolson scowled. "You'd think he'd have given up this nonsense by now." He studied Julia through squinting eyes, pushing himself closer to her. "I should give you my condolences."

Julia glared at him. "So, you knew my mother."

He shrugged. "She married my son."

"Who you killed," Julia snapped.

David Kolson's bottom lip began to quiver and his voice cracked, when he said, "Please sit down. I'd like to talk with you."

"I'm not going to promise to keep any secrets, Mr. Kolson," she said.

The old man sighed and rolled himself near a couch. Julia went over and sat down.

"We're done with these secrets, Julia," he said. "I'm old, tired."

Julia noticed that his hands had a slight tremble.

"That Jack Landry of yours has been a pain in the ass for the last few years, but nothing we couldn't handle...until he found you."

"He wasn't looking for me," Julia said. "He just happened to overhear me say I was looking for Dennis Kolson, my father."

David Kolson dropped his head to his chest. He appeared to be crying. Julia didn't know what to do, but she certainly didn't feel like comforting him.

He came up for air, pulled a handkerchief from his pocket and began dabbing at his eyes. "He was a troubled young man. I should have seen the signs when he was just a boy."

"What kind of signs?" Julia said.

"Oh, I don't know. Now when I say it, it seems I was foolish not to have gotten him the help he needed before...before..."

"Before he got killed in the hunting accident?" Julia said with a sneer.

David Kolson sputtered. "It was like one of those Russian dolls, one lie leading to another, except going from bigger to smaller, it went the other way."

"So, it wasn't a hunting accident?" Julia said.

His eyes red, he said, "Have you ever met someone with psychosis?"

Julia shook her head. "No, not that I know of."

He mulled it over, and then said, "Well, I never thought so, either, but here I had a wife and a son with that damn illness."

Julia leaned in. "Your wife was psychotic, too?"

"She's in Belmont, here in Philadelphia."

"She's still alive? But I thought---"

"That she was dead? Another lie. We decided that the media didn't need to know so we conjured a lie that she had cancer. When she died," he said, making air quotes with his stiff fingers, "we had a closed casket so no one would know. Had the burial and everything."

"Isn't that illegal?"

"You'd be surprised how many people are willing to be paid off to keep quiet when they know there's money involved."

"My mother being one," she said.

"Thing is, your mother didn't realize that my son should never have been let out of that hospital. Not for one minute."

"So why was he?"

"Damned if I know," he said. "If they'd asked me, I would've told them about the little boy who liked his pets. He would be obsessed with his cats and dogs, kept him with him night and day. But when they wanted to prowl or do what dogs and cats do, he had none of it. He'd tell us that they ran away, but we found out otherwise."

"What do you mean?"

"He'd kill them. He was creative in how he did it. He said that they stopped loving him and didn't deserve to live any longer."

Julia fell against the back of the couch, shocked. "But why are you telling me this now?"

"Because your Jack finally managed to unweave the stories and lies, and it's time for the truth."

"What do you mean?"

"We were informed this morning that he filed a report with the police."

"So you do know where he is."

"I was just informed by my son about the report this morning. Your Jack found out that his aunt's accident was actually murder. But he was wrong about the murderer. It wasn't Dale or Donald."

"Another lie?"

"Dennis killed Katherine."

Julia had to catch her breath. "But that's not possible. She was the love of his life."

"Just like all those cats and dogs," David Kolson said.

It took a minute for Julia to absorb that thought before she said, "I'm amazed he didn't kill my mother."

He shrugged. "Why would he? He never really loved her. From what I could tell, he manipulated her to somehow get him out of that hospital. She gave him a place to stay, until he decided to show up at my door and try and blame his brothers for killing Katherine. That's part of being psychotic. Delusional."

She leaned in. "So how'd he die? Really?"

David Kolson looked her straight in the eye. "Dale killed him, but it was in self-defense. There was no reasoning with Dennis then. He kept saying that he was going to go to the media, tell them that Dale had a hand in Katherine's murder; tell them that we killed his mother."

"But you would have been able to prove that he was making it all up."

"My son, Dale, wanted to be the next John Kennedy, Julia. He had political ambitions. If Dennis put that seed of doubt in the minds of those against us, they would have wanted to exhume Susan's body."

"Susan was your wife, right?"

"Is my wife. She's still alive, remember? And imagine what would have happened then. And if Dale had proven that he had nothing to do with Katherine's murder, there would still be doubts in people's minds." He stopped for a minute, putting his handkerchief back into his pocket. "Ever hear of Mary Jo Kopechne?"

Julia shook her head.

"She drowned; the car she was in went off a bridge. Very similar to Katherine's."

"I don't get the connection."

"Ted Kennedy was driving that car. He survived, she didn't. His ambitions to become president were ruined that night. Even though he gave a statement about what had happened that night there were too many questions unanswered. My son isn't a Kennedy and didn't have the connections they did. He would have never gotten anywhere."

"Your sons told me Katherine was a gold digger. That she was trying to get to your money through Dennis. That she was pregnant with his baby."

"Sometimes my sons speak before they think. They were trying to cover up for their little brother."

"So they knew he killed her?"

"We suspected it was a possibility, which is why we shipped him off to Pilgrim State. We had to keep him quiet and try to get him better."

Julia found the information too much to take while she had so many more questions. "You said on the phone the other day--when you thought you were talking to my mother---something about next year being important."

"I was talking to you then, wasn't I?" he said.

"You were."

"Well, it doesn't matter anymore. Dale's going to have to go back into real estate. His political career is over."

"But won't he have to go to jail?"

"That's a possibility. But it was in self-defense. Dennis had every intention of killing Dale, but what political family wants the bad press; the questions that would lead to more questions? It's why I had to give up on any thoughts of taking that career path myself. I knew Susan would never be able to handle being the wife of a politician. She was just too unstable. And by the time we had her admitted in to Belmont, it was too late for me."

Just then there was a light rap at the French doors.

"Come in," David Kolson called.

Karen came in, carrying a glass of water and some pills. "Time for your medicine, David," she said.

"Damn blast it," he said. "Goddamn pills all the time."

Karen looked at Julia and rolled her eyes. She said to David, "Now stop your complaining. You know you always feel better when you take these."

After he'd taken his pills, he said to Julia, "Would you care for a drink? Something to eat? Karen can tell the kitchen staff."

"No, thanks. I'm fine."

"Okey dokey," Karen said, leaving the room.

"Mr. Kolson," Julia said, "why did you have John come and get me? Why couldn't you have just asked to see me?"

"Would you have come?" he said.

"Of course, I would have," she said.

"I'm not so sure," he said. "Besides, I wanted to be sure that you weren't bringing Mr. Landry with you. I wanted this to be a tête-à-tête."

Jack's name reminded her that he had yet to call her. She said, "Is he being held against his will?"

David Kolson chuckled. "You are like all of the rest, aren't you? Just because a family has the ability to own businesses and buy real estate, as well as dabble with politics, it doesn't mean we're criminals. So, no, I told you, he's not being held against his will. What is it that they call families like ours?" He stopped to think, his face all scrunched up. "Oh, right, dysfunctional. The Kolsons, yes, are dysfunctional, but that's about it."

"But my mother carried a burden for years to keep your secrets. Why'd she have to do that?"

"She believed Dennis when he told her his brothers killed Katherine, but she also knew that he was a psychopath."

"But why did you pay her to keep quiet?"

"Most of the money your mother had was from insurance policies and what my father had left him in his will. But we're not the cold bastards you take us for. We knew she was pregnant with Dennis's baby and I felt responsible for that. I wanted my granddaughter to be taken care of. If I had to guess, though, your mother was probably more afraid of you finding out about your father's mental illness than anything else."

"But you stayed in touch all these years!"

David Kolson shook his head. "No, no we didn't. She managed to track me down to ask me about Mr. Landry. She was afraid of what he was going to uncover. She was only trying to protect you from the truth."

"And she died doing it," Julia said, her throat closing up.

Suddenly, there was a racket going on out in the hall. The French doors flew open with John pushing Jack into the room.

EIGHT

"Jack!" Julia shouted, running to him, throwing her arms around him. He smelled of perspiration and she didn't mind it at all. "He told me," she said, motioning to David Kolson, "that they weren't holding you hostage! Another lie!"

"Babe, babe," Jack said, taking her face in his hands. "No, they weren't holding me hostage."

"So why didn't you call me back? I left messages for you...and who answered your phone, anyway?"

Jack sighed. "I must've dropped it at the gas station on the way back. I didn't realize it until I was almost in Philly. I couldn't go back for it, and didn't have your number memorized so that I could call from a pay phone. I had to get back here, though, and report what I found."

"So, now that the media and police know everything," David Kolson said, "you must feel quite pleased with yourself."

"Wait, how did you know I was here?" Julia said.

"I didn't. I went to Dale's headquarters after I went to file the report. I decided there was no need to hide any longer. I wanted to be a man and face him. He wasn't there, of course, but the secretary somehow got in touch with this thug and he escorted me here."

"Thank you, John," David Kolson said. "We'll be fine." John nodded and walked out of the room.

"I'm sorry, Julia," David Kolson said, "but we didn't take Jack as a hostage. I did know that he was in town and John was told that if he crossed paths with him to bring him to me. Having you here was just a lovely surprise. It's nice to finally meet my granddaughter."

He turned his wheelchair to face Jack. "Young man," he said, "I need to know-- how did you figure out that Dennis was the one who murdered your aunt?"

"I wasn't a hundred percent sure, but after I found the key to my aunt's vehicle in his possessions and discovered that he'd been in a mental hospital, things started to make more sense. Politics and psychos don't make very good partners."

David Kolson gave a wry smile. "The current situation seems to prove differently."

Jack laughed. "You have a point."

"Well, as I told Julia, I'm tired of all the secrets and lies, especially now that there isn't quite the same stigma when it comes to mental illness. But years ago, we couldn't say the same." He looked over at Julia. "You, young woman, have nothing to worry about. You have much to be proud of."

Barely above a whisper, Julia said, "Thank you."

"I never knew, Jack, why your father hated us so, until he had good reason to. Everyone was busy buying up real estate all those years ago. Okay, maybe I did pull some strings, but I didn't do anything illegal."

Jack glared at him. "At least that could be proven."

"Touché."

"How is your father, by the way?"

Jack looked pointedly at David Kolson stuck in his wheelchair, and said, "He's great, just great. He and my mom have been traveling and enjoying the sunset years of their lives."

David Kolson studied him for a moment before saying, "Very well then. Julia can fill you in on all that we discussed. I've about had it for today."

"Great, but just how do we get back to our vehicles?" Jack said.

"I'll instruct John to drop you off," he said, before shouting as loudly as he could manage, "John!"

In a heartbeat, John appeared.

"Please bring these two back where you found them."

Julia went to grab her purse when she felt a hand grasp her arm. She looked up to see that it was David Kolson. With tear-filled eyes, he said, "It's over now."

She was tempted to hug him, but couldn't bring herself to do so. She pulled away and went over to where Jack and John were standing. Just as they were about to walk out the French doors, Jack stopped and turned. He said, "Mr. Kolson?"

"Yes, Jack."

"You get the Inquirer?"

"Every day."

"Be sure to read it tomorrow. I think you'll appreciate the feature story."

John dropped Julia and Jack off at Jack's vehicle. Jack told him he'd bring Julia to her car.

Once the thug took off down the street in his SUV, Jack pulled Julia into him and clung to her without speaking. It took a few minutes before Julia realized he'd been crying.

"Jack, what's wrong?"

"I lied to Mr. Kolson."

"Oh, I know, honey, but I understand why you did. He doesn't need to know how sick your dad is."

Jack shook his head as if trying to form a sentence. He then blurted, "Dad died. Early this morning."

"What?"

"I called Mom, from the Inquirer office, after I filed the report. I was so happy to have gotten to the bottom of the story and couldn't wait to tell her and dad. Like you, she'd been trying to contact me, too, to let me know. Damn it, what a bad time to lose my damn phone!"

"So your dad never found out the truth?"

"No. And I guess I was saying those things about him and Mom traveling and enjoying their lives as much for myself as to stab him a little."

"So, that story you filed. I'm not sure you have it all," she said.

"What do you mean?" he said.

Julia then explained about how Susan Kolson wasn't dead, but had been kept in a mental hospital for years. Once she finished telling Jack all that David Kolson shared with her, Jack said, "This apparently is going to be a series."

"Wait, I thought the paper let you go. So how were you able to file a story with them?"

"Different paper. I'd been in discussion with the editor at the Inquirer for the last couple of days and filling him in on what I was finding out about the Kolsons. His paper is not a fan of that family so they were more than happy to have me run with the story." They got into his vehicle. "Where's your car?" he said.

"The parking lot down on Maple."

"Would you mind if we go to my mom's? She's got to be a wreck."

Julia didn't think she could handle any more sadness just then, but said, "Maybe she'd rather I wasn't there."

"I want you there, babe. She'll understand."

NINE

Summer was coming to an end and Julia was mentally preparing for the school session.

She'd emptied the contents of her mother's apartment a couple of weeks earlier, finding nothing more that was revelatory—except for a stack of romance novels from the 1970s tucked away in a box.

She couldn't help but think that her mother really did love her father, even if he wasn't capable of loving her back.

She'd also cashed in her mother's insurance policy, paying off the funeral expenses, and investing the rest. She also booked a flight to visit her Aunt Barb during her first winter break.

"Will Jack be coming with you?" Aunt Barb had asked. "I like him a lot."

"So do I," Julia said, "but I'll have to see if he can get away from work."

Jack was back to reporting and writing, but this time for a different Philly newspaper.

Once the first of the three-part series was published, a local television station followed the Kolsons, relentlessly trying to get statements from them.

One reporter, Jack had told Julia during one of their routine nightly phone calls, was filmed standing by Susan Kolson's headstone where the date of her death was chiseled in granite and then in the next frame he was filmed standing outside of Belmont Hospital, reporting on where the woman had been discovered still alive but being kept hidden for years.

"They dug up her grave," Jack told Julia.

"And?" Julia was sprawled \on her bed, wishing Jack were beside her.

"Just as David said, the casket was empty."

"What about Dale? What happened with him?" Julia tried to suppress a yawn.

"I heard that," Jack said with a chuckle. "Well, there's an investigation, but I drove by his headquarters this morning and there's a For Rent sign in the window. I'm guessing his plans aren't going quite as he expected."

"I know it sounds strange," Julia said, "but I do feel sorry for their father. He had a lot to deal with."

"He made some stupid ass choices, though. I mean putting your wife away and locking the key and then pretending to the world that she'd died? Who does that?"

"A desperate man, I suppose," Julia said. "And I am sorry that your aunt got caught up in all of this."

"Hmmm," Jack said in agreement.

"So," Julia said, without trying to sound too pushy, "when will I see you again?"

"When would you like?"

"Right now!" she exclaimed.

He laughed. "We'll have to work something out," he said. "We do have schools in Philly, you know."

"And we have newspapers here, too," she replied. Just then she heard her doorbell ring. She said, "Can you hold on? Someone's at the door."

"No problem," he said.

She slipped into her bathrobe and went to the door. Keeping the chain lock on, she opened the door a crack enough to see who would be interrupting her evening.

There stood Jack, holding up a copy of Newsday, Long Island's paper.

"So guess who hired me," he said, wearing a bit smile.

The chain lock came off with Julia swinging open the door. She jumped into Jack's arms, finally believing in second chances, and not feeling crazy for doing so.